the torturer's daughter

ZOE CANNON

First Paperback Edition: December 2012

ISBN: 978-1481030786

Cover Art:
Phase4Photography / Bigstock.com

Cover Design:
Zoe Cannon

For Kylen
who never doubted I would make it here

chapter one

Becca's steps slowed as she approached Processing 117. The floodlights of the parking lot shone down on her, exposing her. Past the lot, the darkness threatened to close in. There was no other source of light nearby except for the dim glow of the streetlamps, nothing but trees for at least a mile in every direction.

The concrete structure loomed taller than its five stories—maybe because of the invisible presence of the underground levels, or maybe because in a moment Becca was going to have to walk inside.

Heather can't have been arrested. If she were a prisoner, they wouldn't have let her call.

But when Becca remembered the panic in Heather's voice, the thought wasn't all that reassuring anymore.

Becca took the last few steps across the not-quite-empty parking lot. The windows of the upper floors glowed in a patchwork of lights, showing who was working another late night and who was at home sleeping... or down on the underground levels. Becca knew that in one of those dark offices, a phone had been ringing off the hook for the past half-hour, its owner oblivious to Becca's pleas for her to answer, to find Heather for her, to fix this.

Becca reached the double doors of the entrance—and froze. Her heart thudded against her ribcage.

Heather is in there, she reminded herself. *Heather needs me.*

She pulled the doors open and stepped inside.

The doors slammed shut behind her, the noise echoing off the stark white walls. Security cameras stared down at her from the ceiling. The guards, one to either side of the metal detector, pinned her to the floor with their eyes, but said nothing.

Opposite the metal detector from Becca, the room was bare except for a huge metal desk with corners that looked sharp enough to cut. Behind the desk, a dark-haired woman with a headset clipped to her ear stopped mid-yawn and jerked up to face her.

Becca held her breath and stepped through the metal detector. Its light flashed green, and one of the guards waved her forward. She let her breath out and stepped up to the desk.

She eyed the woman's crisp gray suit, and the desk that gleamed like it had never seen a speck of dust in its life. Then she looked down at her own clothes, the jeans and wrinkled t-shirt she had grabbed from her dresser after hanging up with Heather. She crossed her arms around her stomach.

The receptionist's bleary surprise had vanished, replaced by a stone mask. "Can I help you?"

"I'm looking for…" Becca bit back the name on her lips. No. If she were in her office, she would have answered the phone. Anyway, Becca could imagine her reaction at finding out about this midnight walk to 117. Becca was on her own.

"…Heather Thomas," she finished. "She called me half an hour ago and told me she was here."

The receptionist's expression didn't tell Becca anything.

"She's here… somewhere… she called me…" Becca's voice trailed off. *I'm not doing anything wrong*, she told herself. *I'm not a dissident. Heather's not a dissident.*

Which led Becca back to the question that had been circling through her mind since she had gotten Heather's call. What was Heather doing here?

The receptionist turned away and tapped something out on her keyboard. It only took her a few seconds to find what she was looking for. She typed in something else and touched her earpiece. "We have a detainee in temporary holding," she said to someone Becca couldn't see. "Last name Thomas. Her file says she's waiting for a relative to collect her. Right, that's the one. Someone forgot to collect her phone, and she called a friend." A pause. "No, that won't be necessary. Just confiscate the phone."

She turned back to Becca. "Heather Thomas is waiting for her guardian to arrive. Are you Lydia Thomas?" She gave Becca a skeptical once-over.

Becca considered saying yes, but even if the receptionist weren't going to ask for proof, there was no way she could pass as Heather's… aunt, she remembered after a moment. Aunt Lydia, the one who always looked at Becca and Heather like being in high school was catching.

The receptionist took her silence as an answer. "I'm going to have to ask you to leave."

Becca wanted nothing more than to do just that. But she couldn't leave and let this place swallow Heather. "If she's waiting for her aunt to get here, I can wait with her until she shows up."

"I'm sorry," said the receptionist, already turning back to her computer. "The policy is clear. The detainee will remain in temporary holding—alone—until her guardian arrives."

Becca was losing ground. And somewhere in this building, Heather was waiting for her. "I'm not trying to take her home or anything. I only want to…" To make sure she wasn't locked away underground. To make sure they hadn't gotten her mixed up with somebody else, some dissident slated for execution. "…to let her know I'm here. I promised her I'd—"

"Your refusal to leave the building when instructed will be recorded." The receptionist placed her hands on her keyboard. "May I have your name?"

"At least tell me what happened. Why is she here? Is she all right?"

"Your name, please," the receptionist repeated.

If she stayed much longer, the receptionist would order the guards to drag her out—or worse, in. She could end up in one of those underground cells… She shivered. They couldn't do that to her just for asking about Heather, right?

"Your name," the receptionist repeated again, with a glance toward the guards.

Becca slumped. "Rebecca Dalcourt."

The receptionist blinked.

"Well," she said, her voice suddenly warmer, "I suppose we

can make an exception."

* * *

The room looked like somebody's afterthought. The walls were painted a flat gray that matched the worn carpet. Two folding chairs had been shoved together along one wall, leaving the rest of the room empty. The smell of sweat and carpet cleaner hung in the air. Heather sat in the chair furthest from the door, rocking slightly. She didn't show any sign of having heard the door open.

The guard stepped out of the room and pushed the door shut behind Becca. It closed with a click that made Becca suspect she was now locked in.

"Heather?"

Heather didn't look at her.

"It's me. Becca. I told you I'd come."

Heather raised her head like she was moving through water. She stared past Becca with mascara-smeared eyes. Her hands trembled in her lap. This wasn't the Heather who had tried to talk Becca into a makeover at the mall this afternoon—or was that yesterday afternoon by now? She could still hear Heather laughing as she tugged Becca toward the makeup counter. *Come on, Becca! Do something fun for once.* The girl in front of her looked as if she had never laughed in her life.

Becca sat down next to the trembling girl who didn't look nearly enough like Heather. "What are you doing here?" Her voice came out as a croak. She cleared her throat. "What happened?"

On the phone, Heather had only managed disconnected phrases through her sobs. *Took them. Told me to wait. Please come.*

Please. And then the words that had chilled Becca's blood and brought her here—*I'm at 117.*

Now Heather dug her nails into her legs as she spoke. "My parents." She swallowed, like she was trying to take back the words before she could speak them. "Internal took them."

"What do you mean, took them?" Stupid question. That only ever meant one thing. But... Heather's parents, below them in one of the underground cells? No. Heather's parents had worked for Internal Defense longer than Becca had known them, longer than Heather had even been alive. For them to be arrested... how could Internal have made a mistake like that?

Heather sank bonelessly back against the chair. The back of her head thunked against the wall; she didn't seem to notice. "I don't know why... I don't know why they..."

"Tell me how it happened." Maybe Heather had gotten it wrong. Impossible, to get something like that wrong—but more likely than Heather's parents being dissidents.

"I heard footsteps. After Mom and Dad were asleep. I was still up." Heather dug her fingers deeper into her jeans, until her nails went white. "I thought it was a burglar or something. But it was... them."

"Enforcement?" Becca tried to imagine Enforcers in Heather's apartment, with their faceless helmets and black body armor, dragging Heather's parents away like dissidents in the middle of the night. She couldn't.

Heather nodded. "They walked past me like I wasn't there. They got Mom and Dad out of bed. I didn't know if I should warn them, or... It didn't make sense. None of it made any sense." Heather paused to catch her breath. "Mom tried to fight. They slammed her against the wall a couple of times. I

- 6 -

think her nose was broken, after. I don't know."

Heather stopped, blinking back tears. Becca waited.

After a moment, Heather continued. "She tried to say something to me, but they wouldn't let her. Dad… just went with them. He didn't argue. He didn't say anything. I kept trying to tell the Enforcers they had the wrong people, but they wouldn't listen." Her last word broke off into a sob.

What could Becca say to any of that? She placed her hand over Heather's and tried to ignore the thoughts creeping into her mind, the voice telling her that Heather's parents wouldn't have been arrested if they were innocent.

"It has to be a mistake." Heather's eyes dared Becca to contradict her.

Earlier, when she had thought Heather was the one in trouble, Becca had told herself the same thing. She had worried over all the possible scenarios. Someone could have misinterpreted what Heather had said about not wanting to join the Monitors. Or there was that Monitor who thought Heather had stolen her boyfriend last year—she could have decided to get a horrible kind of revenge. Or Internal could have gotten Heather confused with somebody else.

But all those scenarios applied to *Heather*. Heather hadn't been arrested; her parents had. That changed everything. No one would arrest two Internal agents without double-checking. No one would dare.

Becca had taken too long to answer. Heather's gaze hardened. "You don't think it was a mistake," she accused. "You think they're…" She stopped short of saying the word.

"No!" The denial leapt from Becca's mouth; whether it was for her benefit or Heather's, she didn't know. She lowered her voice. "I'm sure it's a mistake," she lied. "Processing probably figured it out as soon as your parents got here. They'll probably walk in here any second now and explain everything."

The door opened.

Becca and Heather both jerked to their feet. But the woman who stepped into the room ahead of the guard wasn't Heather's mother. She was tall and bony, with a pinched expression on her face. She aimed her gaze at a point above Heather's head like she was afraid to look directly at her.

"Aunt Lydia." Heather's voice was flat.

Heather's aunt turned to the guard. "I assume you've made sure she's... safe."

The guard frowned. "Safe?"

"I'm not bringing a dissident into my home."

"We're not in the habit of releasing dissidents," the guard said stiffly. He gestured to the door. "We have some paperwork for you to take care of, but then you'll be free to take Heather home."

Heather filed out of the room behind her aunt, casting a panicked look over her shoulder at Becca. Becca tried to follow, but just outside the door, a second guard held her back with a hand on her shoulder. "Your friend's aunt is here to take her home. It's time for you to leave."

"But Heather——"

"Will be taken care of. Go home. Get some sleep." He tightened his grip. "I'll escort you to the exit."

It's just a mistake, Becca wanted to call after Heather. *They'll work it out. It'll be okay.* But Heather was already gone.

* * *

The creak of the apartment door woke Becca from her half-sleep. She raised her head to see her mom slip into the apartment. She stood up from the couch, causing every muscle in her body to protest.

Her mom closed the door behind her, then leaned against it and groaned in exhaustion. Only then did she look at Becca.

Her gaze sharpened; so did her voice. "I would have thought you'd be asleep, after your visit to 117 last night—or was it this morning?"

Her mom had found out. Of course she had. But despite her mom's disapproving tone, Becca relaxed at the sound of her voice. Processing was her mom's world; if anyone could fix this, she could. Becca could lay the problem at her feet and go to sleep knowing Heather would be okay.

"Heather called me," said Becca. "I tried to call you, but you didn't answer your phone. Heather's parents—"

Her mom interrupted. "I was on the underground levels all night." She gave Becca a stern look. "You should have waited. I don't like the thought of you walking down that road in the middle of the night—let alone going to 117. If you had waited a couple of hours, I could have told you everything was under control."

"Then you know what happened?" More of the tension slipped out of Becca's muscles. Her mom was handling it. Becca didn't have to do anything else.

"With Heather's parents? Yes." She looked like she was about to say more, but stopped.

The doubts that had wormed their way into Becca's head during her talk with Heather started whispering to her again. She shook them aside. "Why were they arrested? It was a mistake... right? I mean, it had to be." Even she could hear the uncertainty in her voice.

Becca's mom crossed the room to where Becca was standing and sat down on the couch. She motioned for Becca to join her. Becca did, although she wasn't sure she wanted to. A cold knot started growing in the pit of her stomach.

"I knew this wouldn't be easy for you." She had her mother-face on; her voice was heavy. She hadn't sounded like this since the day ten years ago when she had told Becca about the divorce.

She stared ahead of her out the window, where the sky was beginning to show the first glimmers of sunrise. The light glinted off the half-finished new apartment building next door. From what Becca could see so far, the new building would look just like the one she lived in, except maybe a little bigger. In an hour or two the construction noises would start up again.

"We all learn this lesson, sooner or later," she continued. "A neighbor or a friend or a relative is arrested, and we find out we don't know the people around us as well as we thought we did. I wish you didn't have to find out this way."

Not a mistake after all. But how could Heather's parents have been... The cold in Becca's stomach started spreading through her limbs.

Becca shook her head. "You have to tell me more than that. This is *Heather.*" Becca's best friend for ten years, ever since Becca's dad had moved across the country and her mom had moved the two of them to Internal housing—to the apartment next to Heather's.

The day Becca had moved in, Heather had distracted her from her tears by showing her around the building and doing funny imitations of all the neighbors. Before long, they had been over at each other's apartments every day, Heather getting Becca into trouble and Becca getting Heather out of it. Now, ten years later, they were still inseparable—Heather with the spark that drew everybody in, Becca the anchor that held her to the earth. Heather was the one person in the world who knew Becca better than her mom did... and out of all Heather's friends, Becca suspected she was the only one Heather trusted enough to really confide in.

And now Becca was supposed to believe Heather's parents were dissidents?

"All right," her mom said heavily. "You know Heather's parents worked in Surveillance."

Becca nodded. "So they can't be dissidents. If they were, how could they have worked there for that long without anyone knowing?"

"They were very careful," her mom answered. "For most, if not all, of that time, they've been working with a dissident group we thought we eliminated a couple of years ago—a group that had several people inside Internal. Heather's parents have been altering transcripts, deleting data, and passing warnings to suspected dissidents." The weariness in her voice increased with every word. "I know this isn't the answer you were hoping for, but they are dissidents."

Becca quieted the voice in the back of her mind that told her Internal almost never got it wrong. The voice that reminded her how Heather's parents had encouraged Heather not to join the Monitors, and how they always got quiet when the news came on. "How do you know for sure it was them doing all this, and not somebody else? That's happened before. You've told me." Becca stood up. "Did you look into it? Can't you try to figure out what happened?"

"Sit down, Becca. There's something else I need to talk to you about." Her mom sounded more like a capital-M Mother, and less like herself, with every word.

Becca sat down.

"It's about Heather. Children from dissident families..." She shook her head. "There's not much we can do with them. The options are to arrest them along with their parents, or let them go and hope their parents' ideology didn't get passed down to them. A futile hope, in too many cases."

Becca's eyes narrowed. "Heather is *not* a dissident." This wasn't what was supposed to happen. Her mom was supposed to find out what had gone wrong and fix it. She wasn't supposed to say Heather's parents were dissidents. She wasn't supposed to practically accuse *Heather* of being a dissident.

"Unfortunately, there's no way to know for sure. The odds aren't good. And the directors have been telling us to ease up on dissidents' families lately—some new initiative or other—so she wasn't even sent down for questioning. If they would just let us do our jobs..." She shook her head. "So for now, I'd prefer it if the two of you saw less of each other."

Like Becca was going to abandon her best friend right when Heather needed her most. "You didn't answer me. How do you even know this isn't all a mistake?"

Becca's mom looked away. "Because they've confessed. They were assigned to me; that's why I had to work through the night. I heard their confessions firsthand."

Silence echoed through the room.

Becca stood again. "I need to go get some sleep. I'm going to have to get up for school soon."

"If you want to talk some more—"

About what? Heather's supposed secret life as a dissident?

Her mom in an interrogation room with Heather's parents? "Not right now. I need to think."

Becca's mom opened her mouth as Becca stumbled out of the room and down the hallway. Becca closed her bedroom door behind her before her mom could say anything else.

chapter two

As Becca struggled to stay awake during her morning classes, the whispers floated in the air around her. *Her parents. Last night. I heard Becca Dalcourt made them let her go—you know who her mother is, don't you?*

Becca tried to block out the whispers and the stares. She looked for Heather in the halls, but didn't see her. How was Heather handling this? Heather, who had come to Becca in tears last week after someone had started a rumor about her cheating on a geometry test.

When she walked into the cafeteria, everyone's head swiveled toward her. The room's constant roar of conversation dropped to a murmur. She thought she heard her name a few times, along with Heather's. The force of all those eyes and all those whispers felt like enough to melt her into the ground, but she wasn't that lucky.

She almost turned around right then—she could spend lunch in the library. But the thought of Heather facing this alone made her stay.

She scanned Heather's usual table, filled with the school's elite. Heather wasn't there. Maybe she had skipped school... or maybe—Becca's chest tightened—Enforcement had gone back for her. But no, there she was, by herself at a table in the corner, hunched miserably over her lunch tray.

Becca had already played a major part in a lot of the stories making their way around the school this morning. If she sat at Heather's table she would practically be announcing herself as a dissident. And her mom had told her not to spend time with Heather...

It only took her a second to decide. She crossed the room and set her lunch bag down beside Heather's tray.

To the people who didn't know her, Heather probably looked as polished as ever. But Becca took in the wrinkles in her shirt, her hastily-brushed hair, the dark circles under her eyes.

Heather gave Becca a tired smile that dissolved halfway through into a near-sob. She turned her head away and poked at the congealed turkey on her tray. "Thanks for sitting with me."

"I went to 117 for you. You think I'd abandon you now? This is nothing." She slid into the chair next to Heather. "Besides, it's not like I believe any of the stuff they're saying. You're not a dissident." She wasn't. No matter what Becca's mom said. Her mom didn't know Heather like she did. And anyway, her job was bound to make her paranoid about that kind of thing.

Heather made a strangled noise at the last word. She

swiped her hand across her eyes, but not before Becca saw the tear that had started running down her cheek.

The last time Heather had cried in the cafeteria was when her boyfriend of six weeks had dumped her for some freshman. Becca had sat picking at her lunch, separated from Heather by the backs of everyone who wanted to win points with her by offering her a tissue at just the right time or coming up with the perfect insult for the boy in question. That night, Heather had slept over, and she and Becca had stayed up all night talking and ceremoniously tearing up Heather's few pictures of him. The next day Heather had been her usual self again, eyes sparkling as she painted her nails candy pink and wondered aloud how long it would be before her ex realized what he was missing.

Becca wished she could believe it would be that easy this time.

She glanced over at their usual table. At least sitting in exile with Heather meant she didn't have to sit at that table and endure another lunch period of subtle snubs from Heather's friends. A rush of shame followed on the heels of that thought. Heather had lost everything, and this was what Becca thought about?

As soon as Becca looked at them, Heather's friends—probably ex-friends now—all snapped their heads forward, trying to pretend they had been focusing on their lunches the whole time. Becca hoped they all got whiplash.

It wasn't just that table, either. Everywhere she looked, eyes darted to her and Heather, and then away. A black-haired boy two tables away met her eyes when she caught him staring. She couldn't read his intense expression. For a minute Becca thought he might get up and come over to them, but he stayed where he was, dropping his gaze to his tray.

"What do you think is happening to them?"

Becca turned back to Heather. "Who?"

Heather shoved the turkey around some more. "My parents."

Becca knew all the reassuring things Heather wanted to hear. She couldn't say them. How could she, when she knew they weren't true?

Two trays hit the table, saving Becca from having to answer. Anna and Laine slid into the seats across from Becca and Heather. Unlike the rest of Heather's friends, they were Becca's friends too, and they weren't as quick to strike when they smelled blood in the water. Becca should have known they wouldn't turn on the two of them like everyone else. Becca shot them a grateful smile—both for saving her and, more importantly, for braving the cafeteria's hostile eyes to support Heather.

Anna opened her mouth before she had fully made it into her seat. "Is it true? Are your parents really... you know..." She waved her hand in a vague gesture.

"They were arrested," Heather mumbled, not looking at either of them. "They aren't dissidents. It was a mistake." She stabbed a slice of turkey with her fork.

Anna turned to Becca. "You were there, weren't you?" Her words tripped over each other in their rush to leave her mouth. "Did you really get them to let Heather go? How did you do it?"

Becca was starting to feel sick—and it wasn't from the smell of Heather's lunch. She pushed her own untouched lunch away.

Next to Anna, Laine held herself rigid, like she was afraid

Heather would start spouting dissident propaganda at her. She uncoiled long enough to speak. "If they aren't dissidents, why were they arrested?"

Heather examined her lunch. "I don't know."

"You might not even know if they were," Anna pointed out. "I mean, it's not like they'd talk about it."

"And if she did know," said Laine, pointedly looking away from Heather as she spoke, "why would she tell us?"

Becca met Laine's narrowed eyes. "What are you trying to say?"

"You have to admit, it doesn't look good." Laine fingered her Monitor pin, a small golden shield with an eye in the center, conspicuously.

A few years ago, only the really political kids and the ones angling for good Internal jobs after graduation had become Monitors, or so Becca had heard. Then a group of the most popular seniors got political and joined. After that, pretty much everyone in the school's inner circles signed up every year to observe their fellow students for Internal—but Heather hadn't. Not as a freshman, not as a sophomore, and not this year as a junior.

Becca hadn't joined either. She probably wouldn't have even if she had been popular enough that people expected it. Her mom was already pressuring her enough about getting a job with Internal after she graduated. If she joined the Monitors, it would be like giving in and saying she was going to follow in her mom's footsteps. So she couldn't blame Heather for making the same choice. But now, after last night... Laine was right: it didn't look good.

Becca met Laine's eyes and didn't look away. "If you think Heather is a dissident, why are you even here?"

"We came to talk to you." Laine didn't look away either. "We saw you sitting here with her, and, well, you have to know what it will look like if you take her side."

"People are already calling you a dissident," Anna added. "Not that we believe them."

"She didn't do anything wrong." Becca edged her chair closer to Heather's, just in case Heather—or Laine and Anna, for that matter—had any doubts about whose side she was on.

Laine gestured to the poster above her head. "Are you sure about that?"

Don't be fooled, the poster warned. *Dissidents are everywhere.* A sinister smile peeked out from behind a mask. Beside that poster, another encouraged students to consider a career in Internal Defense. Like Becca didn't hear enough of that from her mom already.

Unlike Laine, Anna looked at Heather when she spoke. "We haven't all decided you're a dissident," she said, shooting Laine a brief glare. "We just want to know what's going on. You're our friend. When we heard what happened, we got worried."

Anna's eyes were shining. This had to be the most exciting thing to happen to her in a long time.

Becca felt like she had swallowed sewage. "So you came over here to make sure Heather was okay. It has nothing to do with you looking for gossip to take back to your friends over there."

Becca had trusted them. She had thought they weren't like the others. Most of Heather's friends treated Becca with as much contempt as they thought they could get away with, jealous of her place as Heather's best friend, bewildered that someone who wasn't interested in playing the popularity game was closer to Heather than any of them. But Laine and

Anna had been different. They had been Heather's friends first, of course, but they had been Becca's friends too.

How many hours had she and Heather spent with them? How many inside jokes had they accumulated over the past couple of years? And for what? So that now they could pick at her and Becca while the other vultures kept their distance?

Anna, at least, had the grace to look ashamed.

"We were just trying to help," Laine muttered. To Becca, not to Heather.

Becca sat up a little straighter. "Unlike the rest of Heather's so-called friends, I'm not going to abandon her, no matter what her parents did. You can stay here and eat, and quit accusing Heather of things she'd never do—or you can leave and get your gossip someplace else."

"You know it's only a matter of time before they arrest her," said Laine with a twist of her lips. "You might want to change your mind before then, or you'll be right there with her." She turned to Heather. "It's not enough for you to be plotting God-knows-what with your parents? You have to drag Becca into this too?"

Heather's hands tightened on her lunch tray.

"You should tell Becca the truth so she can get out of this mess while she still can," Laine continued. "You owe her that much. Otherwise she'll be executed along with you and your parents."

Becca stood. "I told you I don't want your help. Either you can leave, or we will."

Laine ignored Becca. All her attention was on Heather now. "I hope they make you watch when they execute your traitor parents. I hope—"

A glob of turkey hit Laine in the face. Heather stood still

for a moment, breathing rapidly, clutching her now-empty tray. She dropped the tray; it clattered to the floor. While Laine sputtered and spat out turkey goo, Heather ran out of the room.

Becca didn't spare Laine and Anna another glance before scrambling out of her seat to follow.

* * *

Becca caught up with Heather in front of the school. Heather was sitting on the front steps, head on her arms, arms on her knees. When Becca sat down next to her, she didn't move.

Becca scanned the area for teachers or Monitors who might spot them outside. It was bad enough to leave the building during school hours; it would be much worse for someone to think she was sneaking off alone with a suspected dissident. She didn't see anybody—just the unnaturally-clean brick walls of the school, and the unnaturally-green grass. The new high school had just gotten finished earlier this year. The walls didn't have that familiar coating of dust and grime yet, and the new grass hadn't had a chance to yellow in the sun.

She and Heather were safe for now. No one was around to spot them.

There would be no convenient interruptions to save her this time.

What if Heather asked about her parents again?

Heather raised her head, revealing her puffy eyes and smeared makeup. "I can't do this."

Becca put an arm around her shoulders. "You did great."

"Last night Aunt Lydia kept tiptoeing past the door of the guest room, like she thought she was going to catch me calling my dissident friends or something. Every time I heard her footsteps, I thought it was Enforcement. When I tried to go downstairs to get a glass of water, the door was locked. She didn't unlock it until morning. And then I came here, and everyone..."

Becca's shoulders tightened at the memory of Laine's stiff hostility and Anna's eagerness for a juicy story. "They don't know anything."

Heather stared down at the concrete. "They're my *friends*. I've known Laine and Anna since junior high, and they acted like I was just some *dissident*." She sniffed and wiped her eyes. "Everyone thinks I'm a dissident now."

"I don't." She wouldn't allow herself to doubt Heather. She couldn't. Not when everyone else, from their friends to Becca's mom, had turned against her. Besides, she knew Heather too well to think she could be a dissident. So what if her parents were dissidents? Heather wasn't, any more than Becca wanted to work in Processing like her mom.

"And if people can't even see that I'm a good citizen, what about my parents?" Heather continued as though Becca hadn't spoken. "I thought Internal had to realize they'd made a mistake eventually. But if my own friends think I'm a dissident... maybe Internal won't figure it out after all. Not until it's too late."

Becca kept her mouth shut. What could she say? That Internal had been right about Heather's parents? That they had confessed to passing information to other dissidents? Besides, maybe there was still some other explanation. Couldn't her mom have... misheard them or something?

Heather stood up. She looked down at Becca, but it was like she was staring through her. "I have to do something."

Becca motioned her back down. "There's nothing you can do. If it's a mistake..." She paused, afraid of the damage even that small amount of doubt could do. "...and it has to be a mistake... Internal will figure it out." She hated lying. But if she told the truth, she would become just another vulture in Heather's eyes, and Heather would lose the only friend she had left.

Right. She was just trying to keep from hurting Heather. It had nothing to do with her fear of how Heather might react. What Heather might think of her.

She believed that about as much as she believed Anna and Laine had only wanted to help.

"Do you think you could talk to your mom for me?" Heather's voice was thready. Her eyes pleaded with Becca. "She'd listen to you. And Internal listens to her. If you can get her to understand that my parents are innocent, they'll have to do something."

Now was the time to tell Heather about the conversation she'd already had with her mom. No matter how much it would hurt.

She looked away. "I don't know if that's a good idea." *Coward.*

Heather's face was white, like all her blood had spilled out of her along with her tears. "Then I have to do it." She turned around and started walking toward the pristine grass.

Becca rushed after her. "Do what?"

Heather didn't look back. "Make them understand. Tell them they got it wrong." She didn't sound like she was talking to Becca anymore.

Becca grabbed Heather's shoulder and spun her around. "Tell who?" she demanded. "Internal?"

Heather's eyes were directed toward Becca, but she wasn't looking at her. "Then they'll know none of us are dissidents. Not my parents. Not me."

It had been hard enough for Becca to get in to see Heather—the receptionist had been ready to treat her as a potential threat until she had mentioned her last name. If Heather went to Internal and demanded that they release her parents... after her parents had already confessed to dissident activity... "They'll arrest you. And then whatever happens to your parents will happen to you. Why would they believe you if they don't even trust your parents?"

Heather jerked away. She started walking again, quicker this time. "I have to try."

Becca tried to grab Heather's shoulder again, but Heather twisted away from her and took off running toward the road.

"Wait!" Becca shouted.

Heather kept running.

There was only one thing that might stop her.

"I'll talk to my mom," she called.

Heather stopped.

She made her way back to Becca, step by tentative step. "You'll make her understand?"

"I'll do whatever I can." And she would—no matter how unlikely it was that her mom would listen. Because if this didn't work, Becca didn't know what else she could do to keep Heather from going to 117.

She held her breath as Heather considered her offer.

The tension went out of Heather's shoulders all at once. "Okay. Talk to her."

"Promise me you won't go to 117 until I talk to her."

Another long hesitation. Finally, Heather nodded. "I

promise."

* * *

Becca didn't see her mom that night, or the night after that. She went to bed in an empty apartment, and woke up to find her mom's sheets rumpled and a frozen dinner missing from the freezer. Same old routine.

A few years ago, her mom had made it home for dinner most nights. But over the years, she had helped make 117 the best processing center in the country—or had done it singlehandedly, the way some people told it. Now, in addition to local dissidents, 117 processed the worst dissidents from all across the country. They came in on windowless trucks in the middle of the night, and disappeared into the underground levels before morning.

Everyone knew about 117. Everyone who worked in Processing wanted the prestige of being assigned there. And the busier the processing center became, the less time Becca's mom had for anything but work.

On the third night, Becca didn't bother to wait for her mom before microwaving a frozen dinner for herself. She picked at the rubbery pot roast as she flipped through channels. Some stupid sitcom. That TV movie about the woman who finds out her husband is a dissident. Executions. A cartoon about a talking dog.

The door clicked open.

Her mom stumbled inside, her face tinged with gray. She gave Becca a tired smile. "Becca. It's so good to see you. You wouldn't believe how busy they've been keeping us." She collapsed onto the couch beside Becca.

Her mom looked much too tired to discuss Heather's parents. Heather would understand if Becca had to wait another day. Becca could even say her mom had stayed at work all night.

No. She had promised. And if she waited too long, Heather might get impatient and go to 117 anyway. This conversation had to happen now. Becca sighed in resignation.

"What's wrong?" Her mom watched her through half-closed eyes, her head resting against the back of the couch.

Becca ignored the temptation to say "nothing," escape to her bedroom, and forget her promise to Heather. Her mom wouldn't believe her if she said nothing was wrong, anyway. "I need to talk to you about Heather's parents. I know what you said before, but isn't there still some chance you got it wrong?"

Her mom closed her eyes all the way. Her frown lines grew more pronounced. "We had this conversation, Becca."

"Can't you at least look into it? Look at the evidence. Look at who turned them in." The image of Heather striding into 117 demanding her parents' release haunted Becca, giving her voice urgency. "If you don't find anything, you're not any worse off, and if you do, you'll have saved two innocent people."

"Listen to me." Her mom opened her eyes and looked at her. Becca hadn't noticed before how pronounced the dark circles under her eyes were. "I know how hard it is to learn something like this about people you were close to. But you're going to have to accept it." She folded her arms across her chest. Conversation over.

But it couldn't be over. Not yet. "Please. I promised Heather I'd—"

Her mom's brow furrowed. "I told you how I feel about you spending time with Heather in light of all this."

"I can't just abandon her. She's my best friend. And she doesn't have anyone else right now."

Her mom rubbed her temples. "In addition to your safety, you have to consider how this could affect your future prospects. You're graduating next year. If Heather is arrested for dissident activity, a close association with her could seriously harm your chances of finding a good position with Internal."

"I'm not interested in working for Internal." Becca wasn't going to let her mom sidetrack her with this old argument. "Please just say you'll look into it. Do it for me."

"Becca." Her mom rested a hand on her arm. "It's over."

"You could have misunderstood them." She was reaching now, she knew. "Or maybe they—"

Her mom held out her other hand to stop her. "Becca... I executed them the night they were arrested."

The ground dropped away underneath her. Her vision blurred as the room spun.

"It was necessary. They didn't know as much as we had hoped, so we didn't make much progress in finding the other members of their group. There might still be dissidents inside Internal. If we'd waited any longer, they could have been rescued."

I talked to my mom like you asked, but she couldn't get your parents released, because she had already killed them. Hysterical laughter rose in her chest.

"Becca. Say something." Her mom's hand tightened on her arm.

Becca struggled to bring the world back into focus. "It's

okay." She cleared her throat. "It's okay. They were dissidents, right? So you had to do it."

Her mom still looked concerned. "It's understandable for you to have trouble with this."

"Was it…" Becca gestured toward the TV. Most dissidents were shot without ceremony on the underground levels of 117, but some executions were televised, the dissidents confessing their crimes into the camera before they died. Sometimes the executions were replayed for days afterward. When she had flipped through channels earlier, had she narrowly avoided seeing Heather's parents die?

Her mom shook her head. "Considering the Thomases' former positions in Surveillance, Public Relations wanted to keep the details quiet."

Good. At least there was no chance Heather had seen it.

"Are you sure you're all right?"

"I'm fine. Really." What else had she expected? As hard as it was for Becca to believe, they had been dissidents. They wouldn't have confessed otherwise. What was her mom supposed to do, let them go anyway just because their daughter missed them?

Becca pulled her arm into her lap, away from her mom's hand.

She understood. She did.

But what was she going to tell Heather?

chapter three

Becca had never been so grateful for a weekend in her life.

But the two days passed too quickly, and before Becca had gotten past *There's something you need to know* in her imagined speech to Heather, it was Monday morning again.

Avoiding Heather before lunch wasn't hard. The only class they had together this year was Citizenship, in the afternoon. But when lunchtime came around, she stood in front of the cafeteria doors for a full five minutes as the river of students flowed around her. Two choices—sit with Heather and answer questions about her conversation with her mom, or sit someplace else and let Heather think she had abandoned her along with everybody else.

Or option three—skip the whole thing. She turned around. She wasn't hungry anyway.

"The smell of the meatloaf scared you away too?" a voice behind her asked.

Becca spun around. It took her a moment to figure out where she recognized the boy from. It was the hair that did it—the black hair falling into his face. He was the one who hadn't looked away when she had caught him staring on that first awful day.

Now he smiled, a slow smile that filled up his entire face. Becca made herself remember that he had been one of the gawkers that day, craning his neck to get a glimpse of Heather's tragedy. She didn't smile back.

"Where are you headed?" he asked.

Becca shrugged. "I don't know. The library, I guess."

"Good, me too." He started walking. Now that Becca had said she was going to the library, she had no choice but to walk there with him.

He moved clumsily, like he had only recently gotten tall and hadn't quite realized it yet. "I don't blame you for not wanting to eat in there," he said. "I've seen the way everyone looks at you and Heather now."

"It's not like you weren't watching too." She studied him out of the corner of her eye as she spoke, trying to figure out who he was. He had to be new; she hadn't seen him around here before that day in the cafeteria. But something about him made her certain she knew him from somewhere.

He looked faintly embarrassed. "I heard the rumors like everyone else. I wanted to know what was going on. It took me a while to figure out they were all going after your friend for no real reason."

He started up the stairs. Becca followed him, struggling to keep up with his long-legged stride. "What changed your mind?"

"Everyone has a different story about the two of you. All anybody really knows is that Internal took her parents. And having dissident parents doesn't make you a dissident."

Becca wished more people saw it that way. Weird, though, that this stranger would, when none of Heather's friends were willing to stand by her. So did he know her and Heather from somewhere? The more she talked to him, the more she got the sense that she should remember him.

"Do you mind if I ask you something?" she asked as they walked. "Don't be offended, okay?"

They reached the top of the stairs, directly in front of the library. He stopped outside the door. "Go ahead."

"Are you new here, or do I know you?"

"I'm new." He smiled again. "I'm Jake, by the way."

Becca let her breath out. "Good. I haven't forgotten you, then. But…" She frowned. "You still seem familiar. Are you sure we haven't met before?"

"I lived around here a few years ago." His voice dropped as he pushed the library door open. "We went to junior high together. I think you were in my English class."

Jake. Right. She thought she remembered him now—a short skinny kid who had always been joking around. The time away had agreed with him. His chatter that had bordered on obnoxious seemed to have mellowed into a quiet friendliness… and, she had to admit, he was a lot nicer to look at now.

She looked away and hurried into the library before he could notice her studying him.

The library—twice the size of the one at the old high school, with shelves that towered above Becca's head—was empty except for a couple of girls at the computers and a boy with a stack of books beside him. Becca sat down at the nearest table. Jake took the chair across from her.

"You left halfway through the year," Becca remembered aloud. "Actually, I heard——" She closed her mouth before the rest of the sentence could escape. *I heard Internal took you.*

"You heard I was a dissident? Yeah, I've heard that one too." He smiled, as if to reassure her that he wasn't offended. Becca smiled back in relief.

Maybe that was why he wasn't as quick to condemn Heather as everyone else. He'd had his own experiences with people's vicious assumptions. Nothing weird about it after all.

"Well, thanks for not thinking the same thing about me," said Becca.

He leaned back in his chair. "You don't look like a dissident to me," he said with another smile.

Wait. He was flirting, wasn't he? She basked in the unaccustomed attention. A wave of guilt followed. Heather was sitting alone in the cafeteria, still thinking she had a chance of getting her parents back, and Becca was in the library flirting with a boy. Some best friend she was.

"Is something wrong? You look upset."

Becca had missed her chance to flirt back. "Nothing's wrong. I'm just worried about Heather." She hadn't understood until now how much she wanted somebody on her side in all this. Normally she had her mom and Heather—but now Heather was the one who needed her help, and her mom was part of the problem. "I don't know why everyone keeps saying she's a dissident. If she were a dissident, they would have executed her."

"I've heard of dissidents getting released every once in a

while, if they've cooperated."

"That's not what happened with Heather," Becca said sharply. "She wasn't even arrested."

"I'm just saying they might think that's what happened. Or maybe they think Internal let her go so she'd lead them to other dissidents. I don't think they've thought it through that far, though. They're just vultures feeding on someone else's misery."

Hadn't Becca thought of them in exactly those terms, that first day? She really did have an ally—one she never would have known about if he hadn't passed by at exactly the right moment...

How had he just happened to be there?

There was something strange about the way he was looking at her. Underneath his casual demeanor, he was watching her with too-sharp eyes.

She blinked, and it was gone.

Well, of course she was feeling paranoid, after what had happened to Heather's parents. After what she had learned about them.

"Is she doing okay?" asked Jake. "It's got to be tough, going through something like that."

Why did he care so much about Heather, anyway? He didn't know her.

He had that sharp look in his eyes again.

"I mean, she probably didn't even know they were dissidents." He watched her like he was waiting for something.

It was as if someone had dumped a bucket of cold water over Becca's head.

Of course. She should have seen it earlier. She should have guessed.

Jake wasn't interested in Becca. He didn't feel bad for Heather. And he hadn't just happened to show up at the right time.

He was spying for Internal.

The school, like everywhere else, was crawling with Monitors, but everyone knew who they were. Internal needed other people too—people who watched for dissident activity without anyone knowing it. People like Jake. Jake, who had maneuvered her into a conversation about Heather so he could fish for information.

It was bad enough that everyone at school thought Heather was a dissident. If Internal suspected her too, that was a whole different kind of dangerous.

But they had let her go. If they suspected her, why would they have let her go?

It was too easy to think of reasons. Maybe they were hoping she would lead them to other dissidents—Jake had even mentioned that possibility. Maybe letting her go had been some kind of test. Or maybe they just wanted to be sure.

Internal would only need to watch her for a while to realize she was innocent, though. It wasn't as if she would do anything suspicious. Except that it wouldn't take much to incriminate Heather at this point. The way Becca's mom talked about her proved that. All Heather had to do was say one thing that somebody like Jake could misinterpret.

The others might be vultures, but Jake was a predator. He could draw blood.

Jake waved a hand in front of her face. "Becca? You still there?"

"I have to go," she mumbled. She didn't look at him as she hurried out of the room.

Only after the library door closed behind her did she realize how suspicious she had just made herself look.

* * *

Usually when Becca's mom got home early—which these days meant before eight—they had dinner together and spent the evening catching up. This time, Becca told her mom she had already eaten, and holed herself up in her bedroom after a few minutes of small talk. She walled her textbooks around herself and let everything but homework fade to the back of her mind.

Even with her door closed, the doorbell jarred her out of her studying trance. She frowned at her computer screen, trying to pick up her lost train of thought. Her mom could deal with it.

"Becca's not home right now," she heard her mom say to whoever was at the door.

What? Becca scrambled out of her chair and opened her bedroom door just in time to hear the visitor's response.

"Actually," said Heather, "I came to talk to you."

Becca rushed down the hallway into the living room. Heather stood on one side of the door, her mom on the other. Heather's hair was mussed, and her makeup was smudged with tears. Her shirt looked like she had pulled it out of the laundry.

Heather's look of determination changed to a confused frown. "I thought you weren't here."

Becca glared at her mom, who was still standing between her and the door. "I was just in my room."

"You haven't answered my calls."

Becca hadn't meant to keep ignoring Heather's calls. She had just needed more time to figure out what to say. Now, though, her time had run out. "We can talk now, if you want." Becca pushed in front of her mom. She glanced back toward her room—and toward her mom, standing behind her. Too close. Any place in this apartment would be too close. "Outside."

"I don't think that's a good idea," said her mom. "You said you had a lot of homework."

Heather tried to step past Becca into the apartment. "Since I'm here, I might as well talk to your mom myself."

Becca shifted to block Heather's path. "Why don't we go out to the parking lot? We can talk there. It'll be easier."

"What did you want to talk to me about, Heather?" Her mom's voice betrayed only mild curiosity.

Heather took a deep breath. "My parents were arrested a few days ago." She craned her neck to see past Becca. Another breath. "I thought maybe there was something you could do. You know, to get somebody to understand that they're innocent."

Please don't tell her, Becca silently begged her mom. However hard it would be for Heather to hear the news from Becca, hearing it from Becca's mom would be so much worse.

"I'm afraid that won't be possible." Becca's mom sounded distant now. Cold. Becca shivered. She didn't think she'd ever heard that particular tone in her mom's voice before. "I think it would be best if you went home."

Becca shoved her way out into the hall, all but pushing Heather away from the door with her. "Come on. We'll go talk outside." She shut the door behind her before her mom could say anything else.

"What was that all about?" asked Heather as they walked down the stairs.

Tell her what you should have told her on Friday night as soon as you found out. "I asked her about your parents. She..." Becca hesitated. Somewhere, there had to be the perfect way of telling your best friend that her parents were dead, that they had been killed as traitors, that they had been traitors. Becca wished she knew it.

They stepped out into the parking lot. A cool breeze lifted Becca's hair off her neck. The sky hadn't gotten dark enough for the parking lot lights to come on; the red-orange glow of the sunset glinted off the parked cars instead.

"She what?" Heather prompted. She stopped in front of a frighteningly-clean car that had to belong to her aunt.

Becca reached for the door handle, then thought better of it. In the car, no one would be able to overhear them, but how did she know it hadn't been bugged? If Internal was using people like Jake to get information about Heather, there was a good chance they had her under surveillance too.

She sat down on the curb in front of the car instead, and patted the space next to her. Heather joined her.

"She what?" Heather pressed. "What did she say?"

"A boy at school was asking questions about you today," said Becca, instead of answering Heather's question. "I think he's spying for Internal. You should be careful around him. His name is—"

"Just tell me what your mom said," Heather interrupted with an edge to her voice.

Now or never. "She said your parents confessed," Becca began. *Just tell her.*

Heather jumped up, eyes blazing. "Then she's lying."

Becca stood. "She doesn't have any reason to lie."

"Are you telling me you believe her? You think they're dissidents now too?" The rage on Heather's face looked strong enough to eat through Becca like acid. "You're wrong! All of you are wrong." Her voice echoed through the parking lot.

"Quiet!" Becca grabbed Heather's arm. "What if someone hears you?"

Heather yanked it away. "I know them," she said, quieter now. "I grew up with them. They aren't traitors."

If she reacted like this to hearing about their confession, how would she react to the news that they had been executed? What might she say, in her grief and anger, that someone like Jake could overhear?

If Becca told Heather what had happened to her parents, and Heather went to school tomorrow ranting about how Internal had executed two innocent people, and tomorrow night she disappeared, would Becca have killed her?

But Heather was going to find out eventually, whether Becca told her or not. And she deserved to know the truth.

There had to be some way to make this easier. To make Heather less likely to do something stupid once she found out.

She had a thought.

It probably wouldn't work—but if there was any chance at all, it was worth a try.

"Do you have any of your parents' things?" she asked.

Heather folded her arms across her chest. "What does that have to do with anything?"

"I have an idea. For—" Another lie. What was she supposed to do, when she choked on both the truth and the lies? "For proving your parents weren't dissidents. If you have papers of theirs, journals, anything like that... maybe there's something that can prove Internal wrong."

Her voice had dropped to a whisper. She glanced around, out of habit, to make sure nobody had heard. Despite her real motives, talking about proving two executed dissidents' innocence made her skin crawl. That was *dissident activity.*

But if that disturbed Heather, she didn't show it. "Internal had my aunt get my stuff from the apartment after they searched the place. She said she got a few of my parents' things for me when she did. I don't know what she took. It's probably not much. I haven't... I haven't looked through that box yet." She swallowed. "But there might be something useful in there."

"I'll come over tomorrow after school. We can look through it then." Becca reconsidered. "No, bring the box over to my place. Just in case your aunt's house is bugged. No one would dare bug my mom's apartment."

Becca didn't want to find something that proved their innocence. That would be nearly impossible, anyway. Internal would always argue that they had simply covered their tracks well.

What Becca wanted was something that would prove their guilt.

If she tried to tell Heather that her parents had been dissidents, Heather wouldn't believe her. But if there was proof...

If Heather knew her parents had been guilty, the news of their execution wouldn't hurt any less. But Heather wouldn't think Internal had killed her parents by mistake... and so she wouldn't accuse Internal where Jake could hear. Or worse, storm down to 117.

"Thanks for helping me with this." Heather didn't sound quite so panicked now. "Sorry for yelling. It just sounded for a minute like you didn't believe me anymore."

"We'll find the truth together," Becca promised. She felt dirty.

* * *

Heather dropped the cardboard box onto Becca's bed.

One box, not much bigger than Becca's pillow. "Is that everything?"

Heather nodded. "She probably didn't want to save anything of theirs. But she thought I might want a couple of things."

How likely was it that Internal had left something incriminating, which Heather's aunt had then packed up for Heather? Not very. But no matter how small the chance, this was worth it. Becca didn't know how else she could convince Heather that her parents had been guilty.

"It's weird being back here." Heather looked around with longing in her eyes. Becca knew she wasn't seeing the tidy space around her with its pale blue walls, but the mirror-image room on the other side of the wall, the one with clothes strewn everywhere and posters covering every inch of available space. The room that was probably empty by now, its walls slathered with enough layers of white paint to erase all traces of Heather, waiting for somebody new to move in.

Heather brought her gaze back down to the box. "You really think there's something in here that could prove they aren't dissidents?"

Becca shifted uncomfortably. "Maybe. It's worth a try,

anyway."

She sat cross-legged on her bed, facing the box. Her fluffy bedspread crinkled under her legs. Heather joined her.

Neither of them opened the box.

Heather glanced around the room again and pulled her arms into her lap. "You're sure no one's watching us in here?"

Becca felt kind of paranoid herself. They were here to prove two dissidents' innocence. Even if that wasn't Becca's real purpose, it was what she had said they were doing. This could get them both arrested, and here they were talking about it in broad daylight. In Internal housing, no less. This was still safer than doing it at Heather's aunt's house, but it didn't feel that way.

But Becca was willing to bet that wasn't what was really bothering Heather right now. However certain Heather was of her parents' innocence, she had to be afraid of looking through that box, just in case she was wrong.

And if things went Becca's way, Heather's worst fears would come true.

"I'm sure." Becca took a deep breath and opened the box.

Although she had known it was unlikely, she had still hoped the box would be stuffed full of mysterious-looking papers. Or that Internal had left a laptop or something behind—although Becca doubted any dissident would store incriminating information on something so easily monitored. Instead, the box was almost completely empty. Down at the bottom, a miniature photo album lay in one corner, next to a jewelry box and a small notebook. That was it.

Heather slumped. "I guess my aunt thought this was all I would want. Or maybe Internal took everything else." She picked up the notebook. "This looks like it could be a journal.

There might be something in here." She started to open it, but stopped the motion halfway through.

Becca slid the notebook from her hands. "I'll look through it for you, if you want."

"I know they weren't dissidents," Heather said hastily, as though Becca had accused her of doubting them. "I just don't think I could handle seeing their handwriting right now."

Becca opened the notebook.

Birdwatching Notebook, the first page read in Heather's mom's neat script.

She tried to banish her disappointment. Maybe the first page was meant as camouflage. She turned the page. She didn't know what she was hoping to find—a signed confession, maybe. Whatever she was hoping for, it wasn't what she actually found: a page that was blank except for a date from about a year ago and the names of two birds. *Bluebird: Sialia sialis. Barn swallow: Hirundo rustica.*

She flipped through the pages. More dates, more birds. *Goldfinch: Spinus tristis.* On another page, underlined twice: *Mockingbird: Mimus polyglottus.* Useless, unless she could convince Heather it was some kind of dissident code.

"Was your mom into birdwatching?" Becca asked, hoping the answer was no.

Heather nodded. "She put a feeder outside the window and tried to identify all the birds she saw. She got really excited when she spotted one she'd never seen before." Her voice was soft with memory. "Why?"

Frustration built to a pounding point between Becca's temples. "That's what this is. A birdwatching notebook." She set it back into the box, only resisting the urge to hurl it across the room because it probably meant something to

Heather.

Beside her on the bed, Heather was paging through the photo album, slowly tracing each picture with her finger.

Becca pulled out the last item, the jewelry box, without much hope. She examined each edge carefully, hoping for a secret compartment, but found nothing more mysterious than an earring without a mate.

They weren't going to find anything.

She hadn't really expected this to work. Still, the failure tasted bitter in her mouth. After they finished their search and came up empty-handed, Becca would have two choices: tell Heather that her parents were dead and watch her self-destruct, or wait for her to find out some other way and put off the explosion a little longer.

A soft sniff drew her attention. She turned to see Heather wiping away tears as she brushed her finger against the edge of one of the pictures. It showed her parents together, younger, probably before Heather was born. The tears fell faster, and Heather whimpered, like she had forgotten Becca was there.

There was no point in doing any more searching. Dragging this out would only hurt Heather more.

"I don't think there's anything here." Becca took hold of the photo album. Heather didn't resist as she slid it out of her hands. She wished she could say something else, something to ease Heather's grief. But every word of reassurance she could offer would be a lie.

As Becca lifted the album, the picture that Heather had been looking at slipped out and fluttered to the bed between them. A piece of paper, folded in half, followed it.

Heather started to grab the paper, then pulled her hand back to her lap.

Whatever this was, it wasn't the proof of their innocence that Heather was looking for. Nobody wrote out their support for the government and then hid it in a photo album.

Becca picked up the paper and unfolded it. Heather peered over her shoulder at her father's tiny chicken-scratch scrawls. She deciphered the note before Becca did; Becca could tell from her sharp intake of breath.

The note was dated two days before the arrest. It wasn't addressed to anyone. Becca squinted until the letters resolved themselves into words.

New info on false confessions—from conversation between Internal agent and someone from an unknown resistance group (both executed). Can you use this?

Ratio of false confessions to real is high: 4 to 1? More?

All confessions about unified resistance are false. It doesn't exist. That's why we've never been able to make contact. Most false confessions are scripted by Public Relations. They use expendable prisoners. That means most high-profile executions are not from real resistance groups.

This isn't widely known, even in Processing. Only a few handle scripted confessions:

Becca skimmed the list of names, hands shaking. She was about to put the note down when the last name on the list jumped out at her.

Raleigh Dalcourt.

Her mother.

chapter four

Becca left the apartment not long after Heather did. She walked along the road, past the half-finished new building, paying only enough attention to her surroundings to make sure she didn't wander into the path of an oncoming car. She needed to get away. She needed to think.

She needed the playground.

All the old apartment buildings on Becca's street had been demolished a few years ago to make room for more Internal housing. There had been plans to replace the playground down the street from Becca's building, too, but after the park a couple of streets away had put in a fancy new playground, everyone forgot about the old one. Now weeds grew higher than the seats of the swings, and the metal slide had long since turned red with rust. The wooden playhouse to the side of the swing set had a sinister feel to it; whenever Becca walked by it she half-expected a killer to jump out.

This place used to scare Becca. For the past few years, though, she had come here whenever she needed a break from the world.

She needed that now.

She climbed the precarious ladder up to the top of the slide, where she sat cross-legged, watching the grass sway in the wind. The construction noises from down the street provided a background to her thoughts.

The words of the note repeated in her mind. The things Heather's dad had written about so casually seemed impossible to Becca. The idea of Processing scripting dissidents' confessions, faking an entire network of dissidents...

She would have called it dissident activity—what else could she call a plot to make the dissidents appear stronger than they were?—if Processing weren't a part of it. If her mother weren't a part of it.

Of course, all this was assuming the things in the note were true. She had no reason to—

At the edge of her vision, something moved.

Becca jerked her head around to face the playhouse, where she had seen the brief flicker of motion. Whatever it had been, it was gone now. Probably just more paranoia. She looked away, feeling silly.

It happened again. A flash of color between the boards of the playhouse.

She spun her head toward the playhouse again—just in time to see somebody walk out.

She didn't move, didn't even breathe, but the intruder

looked up at her anyway. As soon as she saw his face, she recognized him. Jake. Giving her that smile, the one that made her want to trust him. She wouldn't fall for it this time. She knew what he was.

She couldn't deal with him right now. Not after what she had found.

She returned his smile with a glare. "What are you doing here?"

She knew she should be trying not to look suspicious. But right now she couldn't bring herself to care.

He shrugged. "I just came here to think. It seemed like a good place to be alone."

Right. Like he had just happened to run into her in the hallway yesterday. "You don't need to worry about me getting in your way. I was just leaving." She inched her way back down the ladder, tensing each time it creaked.

"You don't have to go," he said. "Maybe we can finish our conversation from yesterday. You know, since you ran off in the middle."

She stepped off the ladder and onto solid ground. Her headache was starting to pulse behind her eyes again. "I have to get home."

"Maybe some other time, then. I'll see you in school tomorrow, right?"

"I guess." She started walking toward the road. Leaving now would look rude. Maybe even suspicious. But she had to get out of here before she exploded.

Jake stepped in front of her. "Whatever I did, could you just tell me?" His smile was gone now, replaced with perplexed frustration. "We were talking the other day, and everything seemed fine, and then you took off. Now you're acting like

I'm the last person in the world you want to see."

Something inside her snapped. "You want to know what you did? How about flirting with me so you could get information about Heather to bring back to Internal?"

Jake's mouth fell open. It took him a moment to close it again. "Wait. You think I'm working for Internal?"

She had caught him by surprise. Good. "Why else would you have been so interested in Heather? Why else would you have been talking to me in the first place? You weren't being as subtle as you thought you were."

"I'm not working for them. I don't know why you would even think that." He shook his head a bit too emphatically. "Maybe I was asking about Heather because I saw the way everybody was treating her. Did you ever think about that? Maybe I was talking to you because I like you."

Maybe he was telling the truth, and she had misread him. Maybe their conversation at school had been completely innocent. Maybe a boy really did like her instead of Heather for once, and she had screwed up her chances with him by accusing him of being a spy.

How was she supposed to know? How was she supposed to figure out what to believe?

There was hardly any chance he was telling the truth. Becca had only ever had a couple of dates, and never a real boyfriend. When most guys saw her and Heather together, they really only saw Heather. And the others were all afraid of her mom. Why should Jake be any different?

He was probably lying. The way her mom had been lying all Becca's life, if the stuff in the note was true.

"Look, if I got it wrong, I'm sorry. And if you are working for Internal... just leave me alone, okay? Heather's not a dissident. If you thought she was, you should have arrested her along with her parents." She started walking again.

"Wait," Jake called.

Against her better judgment, she stopped.

He jogged up to her. "Maybe we can start over."

She should have kept walking. She didn't want to hear anything else he had to say. She didn't want to try to figure out whether or not he was telling the truth.

"Come out to dinner with me on Friday," he said. "We can get to know each other. Maybe I can convince you I'm not a spy." He gave her a tentative smile.

Her refusal was on her lips—but then she thought about what refusing could mean. Maybe Jake was completely innocent, and all he wanted was a date. But if he really was a spy, she had done too much damage already.

The best thing to do—the only thing to do—would be to go out with him, play nice, and make sure he knew she was a model citizen... while trying to figure out whether he was telling the truth.

Although the idea made her stomach tighten, she nodded. "Okay."

The pulsing behind her eyes got worse as she tried to return Jake's smile.

Just one date. She could get through one date.

She hoped.

* * *

Becca assumed her mom would be working late again. Instead, when she got home from the playground, her mom was sitting on the couch, idly flipping through channels. As the door closed behind Becca, she looked up and set the remote down on the coffee table.

She smiled. "I got out of work early for once, so I thought I'd cook dinner for the two of us. I'm making my macaroni soup. It's already on the stove."

Becca studied her mom and tried to imagine her feeding scripted confessions to dissidents, creating, confession by confession, a country-wide conspiracy that didn't exist.

Her mom frowned. "Are you all right?"

"I'm fine," Becca mumbled. She forced herself to smile. "Tough day at school, that's all."

Her mom eyed her more carefully. Becca imagined, for a second, that her mom could see everything in her mind. She squirmed.

Abruptly, her mom stood up from the couch, betraying her exhaustion with only a slight wince. She started toward the kitchen. "Come help me with the soup."

Normally Becca would have welcomed the rare chance to talk to her mom the way she used to. Now all she wanted to do was get away from her and her probing eyes.

But Becca had heard her mom use that tone before. She knew what it meant. She knew she didn't have a choice.

She followed her mom to the kitchen.

Her mom gave the soup a few cursory stirs. Becca tried to find someplace to stand where she could see the pot but wouldn't get hit with her mom's elbow. Whoever had designed the kitchen in this apartment had obviously never cooked a meal in his life. Becca's mom used to complain about the lack of space all the time, until she stopped having time to cook.

Becca examined the soup to avoid her mom's eyes. "It looks

good," she said, just to give herself something to say. "It should pretty much take care of itself until dinner, shouldn't it? You don't need me for anything."

Her mom turned away from the pot to face her. "I need you to tell me what's wrong."

Becca had known this was coming. Reluctantly, she raised her head. "It's just... Heather's parents. I know you had to do it. They were dissidents." The note had proved it. Her mom hadn't done anything wrong. But the thought of what had happened to them still hit Becca like a fist to the face, the way it always did these past few days when she let herself think about it too much. "But I knew them, and now suddenly they were dissidents all along, and they're gone, and... and you were the one to kill them. And Heather will hate me if she ever finds out." She hoped her mom was too tired to see that she wasn't telling the whole truth.

But her mom was already shaking her head. "I've seen you upset about that. This is different. What's really bothering you?"

Maybe she should go ahead and tell her mom what she had seen, ask her what it meant. Maybe her mom would have some explanation for it. But how could she ask something like that without looking like a dissident? Obviously her mom knew her better than that, but still. That wasn't the kind of thing you just asked.

Her mom sighed. "You never used to keep things from me. We used to talk every night, remember?" She swirled the spoon through the soup. "I miss that."

Becca missed it too. Heather had stopped talking to her parents about anything pretty much as soon as she turned twelve; Becca never had. Instead, their closeness had eroded little by little, not by their choice but by the steady growth of Processing 117.

Without their conversations, Becca felt unanchored. She could always count on Heather to offer sympathy—unless Heather was caught up in some drama of her own—but her mom had a solution for everything.

Becca took a deep breath. "Do you ever... try to get dissidents to admit to things they haven't done? Like being part of a network of dissidents that doesn't exist?"

Her mom drew back sharply. "Where did you get an idea like that?"

She shouldn't have added that last part. She shouldn't have gotten so specific.

Too late to take it back now.

"I can't imagine you doing that," Becca assured her. "I just... I heard something about..." She floundered, unsure how to explain her question.

"What has Heather been filling your mind with?" her mom demanded. She slammed her hand down on the counter; Becca jumped. "*This* is why I didn't want you spending time with her. I knew it was only a matter of time before something like this happened."

An image came to Becca, of her mom calling Enforcement and demanding Heather's arrest. "It wasn't Heather! Heather would never say something like that." Now she definitely couldn't tell her mom where she had found the information, or her mom would know Heather had been with her.

Her mom didn't look convinced.

Had Becca condemned Heather with her question, after trying so hard to keep her safe? "I heard it from... Anna." But she didn't want to paint Anna as a dissident, either. "It's not like she believes it. It's just one of those things she heard. You know how she is." She had told her mom lots of stories about Anna over the years, like how for one whole summer Anna had refused to go swimming because she had heard somewhere that three-quarters of all swimming pools were infested with parasites that could crawl into your brain and kill you. Better for her mom to think the question had come from gullible Anna than from possibly-dangerous Heather.

Becca held her breath while her mom thought about what she had said. She had never been any good at lying to her mom.

But apparently it was enough that she was telling the truth about Heather. Her mom relaxed a little. "I still think your friendship with Heather is a bad idea. But I'm glad to know she hasn't said anything like that." She met Becca's eyes. "If she does, though, I assume you'll do the right thing and report her."

"She won't." Becca hoped her mom wouldn't press her for more of an answer than that, because she didn't know whether she would be lying if she said she would turn Heather in.

Speaking of answers... had her mom ever answered her?

A cold prickle traveled up her arms.

Her mom placed her hands on Becca's shoulders. She stared into Becca's eyes until Becca couldn't look away. "What you heard was a dissident lie. It's a common lie, but it is absolutely untrue. Our job is to find dissidents and keep them from endangering the rest of society. False confessions would be useless to us."

Becca couldn't find any trace of insincerity in her mom's eyes, or in her voice.

She had no reason not to trust her.

So why, underneath her relief, did she still hear the words of the note in her mind, and wonder whether her mom was as good at telling lies as she was at spotting them?

* * *

Heather looked terrible.

She almost fell as she staggered off the school bus. She hadn't done her makeup, and the dark circles under her eyes made her look like somebody had punched her. She hadn't come to school yesterday, and judging by how she looked now, she probably should have stayed home today too.

Becca, who had been waiting by the front doors, pushed her way through the tide of students to get to her. But as she approached Heather, someone shoved herself into Becca's path, separating them. Laine.

Heather started to walk away. Laine grabbed her arm. "What makes you so special, huh?" Her eyes were wild. "What deal did you make to get Internal to let you go?"

Becca's stomach twisted. After the scene in the cafeteria that first day, Laine hadn't done anything more than shoot them nasty looks in the halls. Becca had hoped she was done with her and Heather. Apparently not.

Eyes vacant, Heather tilted her head, like she couldn't quite decipher Laine's words. She didn't try to break Laine's grip.

Becca stepped around Laine to stand beside Heather. "Let go of her."

Laine dropped Heather's arm, but didn't walk away. Her gaze flicked from Heather to Becca. "And you. You're in on it too, aren't you? Otherwise you wouldn't be protecting her.

Did you make some kind of deal too, or are they going to come for you next?"

At least she wasn't trying to recruit Becca to her side anymore. Simple hostility was easier to handle than barbed offers of help.

Another wave of students flowed out of the next bus and around the three of them, many keeping a wary eye on Heather as they passed. Becca grabbed Heather's hand—it was shaking—and tugged her toward the school doors. Laine followed.

"Why didn't you save your parents while you were at it?" Laine yelled over the roar of conversation that surrounded them. "Or did you not care if they died, as long as you could save yourself?"

Why had Laine chosen today to come after them, after days of leaving them alone?

Heather's trembling was getting worse. She stopped moving just inside the doorway. "I'm not a dissident," she mumbled, her voice barely audible over the crowd. "I'm not like them."

Laine's eyes narrowed. "Before, you said your parents weren't dissidents. Now you're saying they're dissidents but you aren't. You can't even keep your own lies straight."

Letting go of Heather's hand, Becca turned to face Laine. "You've made your point," she snapped. "Now leave us alone."

Laine continued as if she hadn't heard. "Everyone is going to think I'm a dissident now. They'll say that if my friends are dissidents I must be too. But you don't care about that, do you? You don't care about anyone but yourselves."

Becca tried to signal to Heather that they should go. Heather kept staring straight ahead, eyes glazed. "I'm not a dissident," she repeated.

"Whatever deal you made, it won't last," said Laine. "Internal won't let a dissident go free for long. You'll end up just like Anna."

Becca froze.

"What do you mean, just like Anna?" Her tongue felt thick.

"You didn't hear? Anna was arrested this morning." Laine's words echoed through the rapidly-emptying hall. "I guess you aren't as safe as you thought." Her smile was like a snake, thin and dangerous. "Think about that while you wait for them to come for you." She spun around and strode away, leaving Becca and Heather standing alone.

chapter five

Becca and Heather pushed their way out of the building that afternoon in silence. The only things Becca could think of to talk about were the things she didn't want to think about. Laine. Her doubts about her mom. What she might have done to Anna.

Heather trudged beside her, blank-faced. She looked worse now than she had this morning, if that were possible.

As soon as they stepped into the sun, Heather stopped dead. It took Becca a couple of seconds to realize why.

Laine was waiting for them.

She met Becca's eyes and took a slow, deliberate step forward. "We're surrounded by dissidents in this school," she spat as she approached. She raised her voice loud enough for everyone around them to hear. "If no one else is going to do something about it, I will."

A few students on the way out of the building paused and glanced their way. Laine looked around at them before continuing. "I don't know what you did to make sure Internal left you alone," she said, her voice getting even louder as she spoke, "but we know what you are, even if they don't."

A few more people stopped to listen. Laine's face lost some of its tension with every new addition to the crowd. She was putting on a show. Trying to prove she wasn't a dissident like Heather. Like Anna.

Anna. What was happening to her right now? What had Becca done?

No. She couldn't think about that. Not right now. Maybe not ever.

"As a Monitor, it's my job to help keep this school free of dissident influences." Laine took a step closer to Heather. "I take that responsibility seriously."

How far was Laine willing to go with this? Becca didn't want to find out. She stepped between Laine and Heather.

"Get out of the way," Laine said. "Unless you're going to defend this dissident." She sounded like a stranger. Had Becca ever really been friends with this person?

Becca didn't move. "She's not a dissident. If she were, she would have been arrested. Do you think you know better than Internal?" Her mouth was dry.

Laine shoved Becca aside. Becca stumbled into one of the boys who had stopped to watch; he pushed her away as if she were contagious. She fell to the pavement, and only just managed to catch herself with her hands.

She got to her feet, heart pounding. Her hands burned.

Laine took another step toward Heather. Heather backed

up until she hit the still-growing crowd. Nobody moved to let her through. Instead they squeezed closer together, trapping her inside Laine's circle.

Trapping both of them.

Laine walked by Becca as if she weren't there. She moved closer and closer to Heather until their feet almost touched. "Are you going to confess? Go ahead. Tell us you're a dissident just like your parents."

Heather cringed away from Laine. "I—I'm not..."

Laine grabbed Heather's shoulders. Her fingernails dug into Heather's shirt. She spun Heather around to face her audience, and addressed the crowd. "You all know what she is. What do you think we should do with her?"

Becca couldn't just stand here and watch this. No matter what Laine and the others might do to her. On shaky legs, she started toward Heather.

Before she had taken more than two steps, someone pushed through the crowd until he was inside the circle. Someone with dark hair that fell into his face.

Jake pulled Laine away from Heather. "What do you think you're doing?" he growled in a voice that made the hair on the back of Becca's neck stand on end. His gaze drilled into Laine's.

Laine took a step back. She straightened, visibly regaining her composure. "Protecting our school."

Jake closed the distance between them again. "You're protecting yourself." His face was just inches from hers. The words overflowed with barely-restrained rage. "Are you afraid everyone will start wondering about you if you don't show them how loyal you are?" His pitch changed abruptly, from a near-shout to a hiss. "Is there something you're trying to hide?"

Laine backed up until there was nowhere else to go. Just like Heather had a moment ago. The circle didn't open up for her either.

"Heather is not a dissident." Jake's voice was low, but it carried easily. "If Internal thought she was guilty, they would have arrested her along with her parents. They didn't. And Internal doesn't appreciate people questioning their decisions. Unless you want to be reported for making false accusations, don't come near her again." His gaze traveled from person to person. "Any of you."

A few of the watchers looked like they might challenge him. But the threat of Internal was greater than any physical threat he could have made. Slowly, the crowd dispersed. Laine shot Heather a glare of contempt before scurrying away.

If Jake was spying for Internal, why would he have saved Heather from Laine?

Jake met Becca's eyes. His smile snapped on like he had flipped a switch.

Right. To make Becca less suspicious. She wished it didn't make sense, but it did.

Unless she was just being paranoid because she didn't know how to deal with the idea that a guy might actually like her.

Anyway, whatever his motives, he *had* saved Heather.

She smiled back. "Thank you." What else could she say? She didn't want to think about what could have happened to Heather—to both of them—if he hadn't intervened.

But when she remembered that growl in his voice, her skin prickled.

* * *

Heather came home with Becca; she said she didn't want to be alone. On the bus, she stared out the window while Becca stayed alert for anyone who might follow Laine's lead. She heard their names whispered a few times, but nobody came near them.

Still, Becca breathed a little easier as soon as they got off the bus and away from all those eyes.

"Thanks for what you did back there," Heather said in an anemic voice as they entered the building.

"I didn't do as much as I should have. You should be thanking Jake, not me." They walked up the stairs side by side. They used to walk inside together like this every day after school, and do homework at Heather's apartment or Becca's. Only two weeks had gone by since Heather's parents' arrest, but the old routines already felt unfamiliar.

"Who was that, anyway?" asked Heather.

If Heather didn't know who Jake was, that meant he hadn't approached her. Good. "He's that guy I told you about before. The one who might be spying for Internal." She unlocked the apartment door and pushed it open.

The old Heather would have been worried, or confused, or curious, or *something*. The new one just nodded. "Thank him for me."

They walked inside.

Not ten feet from where they were standing, Becca's mom had told her she had killed Heather's parents. Becca squirmed as though Heather could see the conversation playing out in front of her.

She had to get out of here, away from the ghost of her conversation with her mom. She hurried toward her bedroom. Heather followed.

In Becca's room, they sat down on the bed together, like they had so many times before. Like they had when they had found the note. Becca glanced across the room at her desk. She had buried the note in the bottom drawer, under a stack of old homework. Even hidden there, to Becca's eye it blazed like a neon sign.

They sat like that for a moment, not quite looking at each other, as the silence grew around them.

Enough. There was too much that she was avoiding, that they were both avoiding. It had to stop.

"We need to talk about..." Becca lowered her voice, even though her mom wasn't home. "About what we found."

Heather went rigid. "You mean, that my parents were—" Her voice broke. "I know, okay? I get it. They were dissidents all along. I don't need to sit around and talk about it." She flicked a piece of dust off Becca's bedspread like it had offended her.

In all her thinking about the note, Becca had barely considered what it meant for Heather. For Heather, it wasn't a source of doubt, but something all too black-and-white. Again Becca wondered: what kind of a best friend was she?

"We don't have to." Becca tried to shift into a more comfortable position. Nothing felt right. "Whatever you want. But just so you know, it doesn't make a difference to me. No matter what your parents were, I know you're not a dissident."

Some of the tightness went out of Heather's body. She lay back and stared up at the ceiling. "It doesn't matter in the end. You might know I'm not a dissident, but everybody else thinks I am. Laine is right—eventually Internal will decide they made a mistake and come back for me. Didn't you say they already have someone spying on me?"

"They can't arrest you just because some idiots at school are saying things about you. You haven't done anything wrong." But neither had Anna. And now, because of Becca's lie, Anna was gone.

Which led her right back to the note, and what it had said. What if Internal didn't care as much about truth as she had always believed?

"The stuff in the note... do you think—" She couldn't force out the rest of the sentence. *I'm just talking to Heather*, she reminded herself. *She read it too. She's not going to turn me in.* She started over. "Do you think it could be true?"

"Of course it's not true!" Heather frowned in confusion. "Why would you—" She jerked up from the bed, her movement so sudden it made Becca jump. "You... you're trying to..." She took a step toward the door, then back toward Becca. "You believed me when nobody else did. You defended me when nobody else would. And now you're turning on me too?"

What had just happened? "I'm not turning on you. Why would you even think that?"

"There's only one reason you would say something like that. You're testing me. To see if I'm a dissident after all." She balled her hands into fists. "I thought I at least had one person on my side."

For a moment, Becca couldn't speak. "You really think I would do something like that?" she said when she had recovered her voice. "We've known each other for ten years! I went to 117 to find you!"

"Only a dissident would think any of that could be true,"

Heather said, like she didn't understand why she had to state the obvious. "But you're not a dissident. So why would you ask me whether I thought it was true unless you were trying to set me up?"

Becca swallowed her angry words. Heather did have a point. Only a dissident would even consider believing what the note had said.

She felt like she was standing on the edge of a cliff, the ground eroding around her.

She shook her head, and the image disappeared. "I wasn't trying to set you up. I promise. I was... confused, that's all. Forget I said anything."

Heather didn't answer.

Becca stayed where she was, quiet, hoping. Like coaxing a wild animal to her hand.

Heather sagged. "I'm sorry. I don't even know why I thought something like that. You've stuck by me since this started, and I..."

"It's okay." With everything Heather was going through, it was understandable for her to get a little crazy sometimes. Besides, Becca would rather let it go than think through the implications of what Heather had said.

Only a dissident would think any of that could be true.

"I was so sure they were innocent." Heather spoke so quietly that Becca could hardly hear her. "If they could be dissidents, anybody could." She took a shaky breath, and another. "I keep thinking about that note we found, and wondering if there's some way we got it wrong. Maybe it didn't say what we thought it said, or maybe somebody else put it there... but I can't come up with anything that makes sense." She fixed her eyes on the carpet. "Not that it matters anymore. They must be dead by now."

Becca would never find a better time to tell her.

The silence stretched on too long. Heather pounced. "You know something."

Becca's heartbeat pounded in her ears. "There's something you need to know."

Heather stumbled back to the bed. She sat at the edge, not looking at Becca. "They're dead." It wasn't a question.

Becca wished she could tell Heather that her parents weren't dead, that someone had planted that note in their photo album, that Internal had let them go and they were waiting for her at home right now. "When I asked Mom about them for you, it was too late. She had already..." Her voice trailed off. Even now that Heather knew, Becca couldn't say the words.

Heather raised her head slowly. "She?"

Too late, Becca saw her mistake.

"You said 'she.' Not 'they.' Not 'Internal.'"

Becca saw it coming in slow motion, saw the exact moment when the realization hit Heather.

"Your mom killed them."

Why did Becca suddenly feel like she was the one who had pulled the trigger? "She had to do it. There was evidence... they had confessed..."

"I've known her for years. I've slept over here hundreds of times. I helped her figure out how to redecorate your room for your birthday last year. And she——" Heather gagged.

Becca placed a comforting hand on Heather's shoulder. Heather jerked away. "How long have you known?"

"A few days," Becca admitted.

"And you didn't tell me."

All Becca's rationalizations melted away under Heather's accusing gaze. "I didn't know how you'd react. I wanted to wait until the right time."

Heather's eyes burned through Becca. "And when, exactly, would be the right time to hear that your mom killed my parents?"

"It's not like she had a choice. They were dissidents!" As soon as she said it, Becca wished she could take the words back.

"I can't stay here." Heather ran for the door.

Becca opened her mouth, but nothing came out. Before she could figure out what to say, Heather was gone.

* * *

Only a dissident would think any of that could be true.

Becca rolled onto her side and pulled her blanket over her head, as if it could block out the words. She had to get to sleep. School would start in just a few hours. She drew the blanket tighter and tried to think about something else. Something that had nothing to do with her conversation with Heather, or the note, or Anna.

Only a dissident would think any of that could be true.

Sleep obviously wasn't going to happen. With a sigh, she stumbled out of bed. Then, with bleary resolve, she strode to the door. As long as she was awake, she was going to answer this question once and for all.

She tiptoed down the hallway to her mom's bedroom. The door was closed, giving no hint as to whether or not her mom was home. If she was, Becca would go back to her room, try to fall asleep, and forget about this idea.

Please be home, she found herself whispering in her mind as she eased open the door.

She peered into the dark room. It took her eyes a moment to adjust. The covers of her mom's bed lay flat, the blankets pulled all the way up to the pillow the way she always left them when she wasn't home. Becca snaked her arm inside and flicked on the light. She squeezed her eyes shut at the sudden brightness, and had to squint until her eyes adjusted all over again.

She didn't let out her breath until she saw for certain that the room was empty.

Still, it took her a minute to move, to make her way across the room to her mom's computer.

She knew her mom had work files on there. Some nights her mom would get home late and then spend a couple of hours poring over prisoner files before finally going to bed. There had to be something on there that would give Becca the information she needed.

She had never betrayed her mom's trust like this before. Had never even considered it.

If the information in the note was true, her mom had lied to her first.

And if it wasn't, it didn't matter what she saw in the files, because her mom had nothing to hide.

Her mom had given Becca her password a couple of weeks ago, just a day or two before Heather's parents had been arrested, so Becca could get some pictures off her computer. She probably hadn't changed it since then. Why would she? She trusted Becca.

Becca sat with her hands poised above the keyboard, paralyzed by what she was about to do. Going any further would be admitting—if only to herself—that she didn't believe what her mom had told her.

Only a dissident would think any of that could be true.

But it wouldn't just be an admission of her doubts. It would also be dissident activity. Accessing an Internal agent's files without authorization—it would get her arrested if anyone found out.

Nobody would find out.

She had to know.

Becca typed in her mom's password, hoping it wouldn't work, hoping her mom had changed it. The password let her in as easily now as it had the last time she had used it.

Her mom hardly kept anything on her computer, so Becca easily spotted the icon that would lead to her work files. She let her cursor hover over it for a second before closing her eyes and clicking. When she opened her eyes again, the Internal logo filled the screen, and a small window in the center prompted her to enter a code. *UNAUTHORIZED ACCESS PROHIBITED,* read the warning below the blinking cursor.

Becca had seen her mom do this often enough. She reached her right hand down to open the top desk drawer, and felt her way past carefully arranged pens and notecards. Her fingers closed around her mom's security fob. She brought it out, her hand shaking.

It wasn't too late to turn back.

She watched the blinking cursor for a second, then typed in the six numbers displayed on the thin silver fob's small display. She held her breath as the window disappeared. The code changed every sixty seconds; what if she had missed the brief window of time when it was valid? Would some alarm go off in Processing if she entered the wrong code? She didn't breathe again until a seemingly endless list of files appeared on the screen.

Each file was labeled with nothing but a date and a long number, with the most current files at the top. Becca's relief gave way to frustration as she scrolled through the list. How was she supposed to find what she was looking for? After all that, she didn't even know where to start. What was she supposed to do, search for "false confession"? Assuming there was even a way to search at all.

She scrolled through yesterday's files, and the ones from the day before, and the day before that. Watching the dates count down to the night that had started all this. The night Heather's parents had been arrested.

The night her mother had killed them.

If she went just a little further down the list, she could—

Bile rose in her throat. She scrolled back to the top and hurriedly opened the first file on the list.

Her eyes glazed over as she scrolled through page after page of information. Internal knew everything about this dissident, from his pets' names to where he had gone to kindergarten. So much information, but none of it helpful to Becca.

Maybe she couldn't find what she was looking for because it didn't exist. Maybe her mom had told her the truth after all.

Maybe she should just assume that was the answer and go back to bed.

She was about to close the file when the next paragraph caught her eye.

Matches 80% of criteria for Public Relations request 10843-A. Requirements: police officer, male, 30 to 45 years old, unmarried. Necessary role: Part of a conspiracy within the local police force to help dissidents escape the notice of Internal Defense. Purpose: The rivalry between the police force and Internal Defense, particularly the Investigation division, is impeding our ability to find and apprehend dissidents. If police officers are concerned about being seen as part of this conspiracy, they will be less likely to interfere with our efforts.

Becca might have stayed frozen there forever if she hadn't heard a key in the lock.

She closed the file and shut down the computer. The security fob was still lying on the desk; she grabbed it and shoved it back into the drawer. She made it to the doorway and flicked off the light just as the apartment door opened.

How would she explain it if her mom caught her in here?

She peeked her head out as far as she dared. Her mom didn't look Becca's way as she massaged her temples. When her mom turned around to lock the door, Becca took her chance. She hurried across the hallway as silently as she could. She counted the seconds—one, two, three, four, five and she had made it. But had she made it before her mom had turned back around?

She drew her bedroom door shut and waited for the knock, for her mom's questions about what she had been doing.

The knock didn't come.

Her mom hadn't seen her.

She crawled back into bed and lay there, heart racing. Trying to forget what she had read.

chapter six

Heather avoided Becca all day at school. Becca saw her once in the hall, but she ducked into a classroom before Becca had a chance to say anything. Becca was pretty sure Heather's next class was at the opposite end of the school from that room. In Citizenship class that afternoon, Heather's desk stayed conspicuously empty, prompting the Citizenship teacher to make a few pointed remarks about dissident families.

Becca needed a chance to apologize. To make things okay between them.

And, more importantly, Heather needed to know what Becca had found.

So when she left the school that afternoon, she passed her own bus and got onto Heather's instead.

She practically tiptoed past Heather on her way to her seat, afraid that Heather would tell the bus driver she didn't belong there. But Heather, intent on scraping a piece of dirt off the window, didn't even look her way.

Becca slipped into a seat two rows back from Heather and across the aisle, where she could watch Heather without much danger of being spotted. Not that she needed to worry about that. Heather stared out the window for the entire bus ride, barely moving except for a slight twitch whenever someone said her name.

If Becca hadn't been watching her so closely, she would have missed the stop. Heather had lived in Internal housing for as long as Becca had known her. Becca had a hard time imagining her living on a quiet street like this, in a little house in a row of little houses, each with its own yard and metal fence.

She squinted. This street looked familiar somehow.

If she didn't move now, she would have to find her way home from the next stop. She hurried after Heather. Heather glanced over her shoulder. Her eyes widened when she saw Becca, but she didn't say anything as they left the bus.

As soon as Becca stepped out onto the sidewalk, she remembered. Of course. That was why it looked familiar. She had spent the first few years of her life here—if not on this exact street, then somewhere in this neighborhood. Her dad had insisted on it. He hadn't wanted to live in Internal housing. Becca could still remember the fights—although the ones about the house hadn't been the worst ones, not by a long shot. Becca could almost see a younger version of herself sitting on the sidewalk with her chalk, driven out of the house by her dad's yelling and her mom's icy words.

Heather's voice jolted her out of her memories. "What are

you doing here?"

"I need to talk to you." First things first. "I'm sorry. I should have told you about your parents as soon as I found out."

"You didn't know what to say. I get it." Heather unlatched the gate and stepped into the yard.

"Wait!" Becca pushed through the gate after her before she could close it. "There's something else I need to talk to you about."

Heather waited.

Having this conversation outside, where anyone could hear them, was a bad idea. But going inside would be worse. At least Internal couldn't bug the yard. Becca glanced around; she didn't see anybody nearby. She stepped closer to Heather so she could talk softly.

Heather stepped back. "So? What is it?"

"I looked in my mom's work files last night." Becca lowered her voice even further, until she was almost whispering. "The stuff in your parents' note… it's true."

Heather's face hardened. She took another step back. "I thought you were done with this."

"You don't understand. I saw it." Becca cast another furtive look around. "The dissident's file had instructions from Public Relations about what kind of confession to get. They wanted him to confess to being part of some conspiracy inside the police force, so the police would—"

Heather cut her off. "I don't have to listen to this." She turned around and started for the door.

Becca followed her. "This isn't some kind of trick," she said, remembering Heather's earlier fear that she was testing her. "I'm just telling you what I saw. I didn't want it to be true, but it is."

Heather didn't stop. She was almost to the front door. Another couple of steps, and Becca would lose her.

"There's more." Becca started talking faster. "A couple of days ago, I asked my mom about what the note said. I told her I heard it from Anna—she knows what Anna is like, so I figured it was safe. The next day, Anna was gone."

Heather paused with her hand on the doorknob.

"There's something wrong here," said Becca. "And you're the only one I can talk to. If I told anyone else about this, they'd report me."

Heather turned around.

"I don't know what kind of game you're playing," she snapped, "but I don't want any part of it. First the thing with my parents. Now this dissident stuff." She blinked away what might have been tears. "You were my best friend. The only person I could really talk to. Now I don't even know you."

She opened the door.

Becca had to get her to listen. "I'm not playing a game with you! I'm sorry I didn't tell you about your parents. But this is real."

"I can't talk to you right now. I just… I can't." Heather disappeared inside the house.

Becca rang the doorbell. Nobody answered.

She couldn't go to anybody else with this.

She rang the doorbell again. Somewhere deep within the house, a door slammed.

Becca fought back her growing panic as she began the long walk home.

* * *

Becca and her mom used to be able to talk for hours. Now Becca couldn't think of a single thing to say.

She glanced up from her plate of chicken. Her mom looked the same. She sounded the same. Like the mother Becca had known all her life. But she wasn't. The person in front of her spent her days forcing dissidents to say whatever she needed them to say, spoon-feeding them the stories Public Relations wanted. Letting them die for things they hadn't done. The mom she knew would never do something like that.

So who was this woman in front of her?

Becca dropped her gaze again.

"Things at work are finally easing up," said her mom. "At least for now. I might even be able to make it home for dinner a couple of times next week, too."

Great. Becca forced a smile.

No matter what those people had done, they were dissidents. Otherwise they wouldn't have gotten arrested in the first place. Maybe it didn't matter what they confessed to, as long as they got what they deserved.

Becca's stomach twisted.

Her mom served herself some salad. "How was school today?"

Hardly anyone called me a dissident today, but now my best friend isn't speaking to me.

Becca poked at her chicken. As much as she wanted to get done with dinner as quickly as possible, she didn't think she could force down a single bite. Her stomach hurt more with every word her mom spoke.

"You don't seem like yourself today." Her mom peered at her more closely. "You're not still thinking about what that friend of yours said, are you?"

Becca flinched at the mention of Anna.

Maybe she should just ask her mom about what she had found on the computer. It might not be as bad as it looked.

Then common sense caught up with her. Asking her mom would mean admitting she had gone snooping through her mom's files. Besides, even if her mom told her the truth, what could she say that would get it to make sense?

The only table small enough to fit in this kitchen wasn't quite big enough to hold their plates plus the serving dishes. Becca's plate clanked against the bowl of salad as she cut herself a bite of chicken. She shoved the bite into her mouth to stall for time. It tasted like sand.

Her mom frowned in concern. "You're not, are you? I thought you knew better than to take something like that seriously."

If Becca denied it, would her mom believe her? Her mom could tell when she was lying.

But what was the alternative? Admitting what she had found?

Becca shook her head. "I know better than that," she agreed. "I'm not a dissident." Her hand was starting to ache. She looked down and saw that she was gripping her fork so tightly the edges were digging into her palm. She let go. The fork hit her plate with a clang that made both of them jump.

"Rumors like that are dangerous," her mom lectured as she cut her chicken. "They may seem harmless, but they can easily allow dissident ideology to gain a foothold in society."

"I told you, I don't even believe it. It's just something—" She couldn't say Anna's name. "Something a friend said."

"I don't want you spreading rumors like that." Her mom put her fork down. "Even if you know better than to believe it, somebody you talk to might not, and you will have helped the dissidents undermine faith in our government."

Of course you don't want me saying anything about it. It's all true. "I wouldn't do something like that." She forced down another bite of chicken.

Her mom studied her. "If that's not what's bothering you, then what is?" She held up a hand before Becca could speak. "Don't tell me everything is fine."

Becca had blamed her mood on the situation with Heather before, and it hadn't worked. What could she say that her mom might believe?

Her mom pushed her plate aside, nearly knocking the platter of chicken to the floor in the process. "We need to do something about this. We barely feel like a family anymore. I never get a chance to talk to you, and when I do, you're keeping secrets."

Her mom had lied to her face, and she had the nerve to complain when Becca didn't tell her everything?

Becca pushed away her own plate. She didn't want dinner anyway. "I'm not keeping secrets."

"Then why won't you tell me what's bothering you?"

"Maybe because the last time I told you something, one of my friends disappeared." Too late, Becca clamped her mouth shut.

The silence stretched between them until Becca could hear her own heartbeat.

New lines appeared on her mom's face. "You need to think about what you're saying, Becca. Anna was a dissident. Her parents were dissidents. The information you gave me helped Internal figure that out. If you regret what you told me, it means you regret helping Internal find three dissidents."

She had to tell her mom the truth.

She could hear Jake's voice in her mind, talking about false accusations. Did this qualify? But Anna's arrest was her fault. She had to make it right.

If it wasn't already too late.

"I have to tell you something." Her mouth was dry. "The thing I asked you about the other day... I didn't actually hear it from Anna. Heather and I were looking through her parents' things, and—"

Her mom shook her head. "I know this is hard for you. First Heather's parents, now Anna. But you did the right thing when you told me what she said. Lying about it now won't help anything."

"But—"

"You need to stop this right now." Her mom's voice was sharp. "Internal found enough evidence to suggest that Anna and her parents were dissidents. Lying to protect a dissident qualifies as dissident activity." She held up a hand as Becca opened her mouth to speak. "I don't want to hear another word about this. Do you understand?"

The doorbell rang.

Becca jumped up from her chair. "I'll get it." She raced to the door and yanked it open.

Jake stood in front of her.

He smiled. "Don't tell me you forgot."

Right. Their date. She smiled weakly. "Of course not."

She looked down at the jeans and wrinkled shirt she had worn to school. Heather would never approve of her wearing something like this on a date, but Heather's opinion didn't matter much to Becca right now. Besides, it wasn't like she cared about impressing Jake.

"Who is it?" her mom called.

At least going out with Jake would get her away from her mom. Becca had never thought she'd see an upside to going out with a possible Internal spy who might be trying to get her best friend arrested. "I have to go, Mom," she called back. "I have a date."

Her mom strode into the living room behind her. "You didn't tell me about this."

Jake backed out into the hallway, giving Becca room to get out the door. "Are you ready to go?"

It wasn't too late to make an excuse and stay home.

And go right back to the kitchen to finish her conversation with her mom.

She gave Jake what she hoped was a convincing smile. "Ready when you are."

* * *

"So," said Jake over the low hum of conversation that filled Lucky's Pizza, "what will it take to get you to believe that I'm not spying for Internal?"

Becca tensed before realizing that he had meant it as a teasing question, not a challenge. She forced herself to relax. She didn't exactly have much practice with this kind of thing.

"You could start by telling me about yourself." She kept her voice light.

The smell of pizza made her mouth water. Her stomach had stopped hurting the second she had left the apartment. Jake might be trying to get her to trust him so she would say something incriminating about Heather, but that was nothing compared to what her mom had done.

And being here with Jake, trying to figure out his true intentions, would keep her too distracted to think about Anna.

Almost every table at Lucky's was full, but Becca only saw a couple of people she knew, and none of them were looking her way. Good. She didn't need anybody to see her out with Jake. She didn't know how they would twist this date into further proof that she was a dissident, but she knew they could find a way.

Wait. The woman at the next table over—was she watching them? Becca tensed and angled her body slightly to get a better view. The woman's eyes flicked from their table to the one next to theirs, to one across the room, scanning each one for a few seconds before moving on to the next. She paused for a few seconds to take a halfhearted nibble of her pizza, then began again. Just a Monitor, then. Becca could see the glint of the pin now. Monitors were everywhere; unlike their counterparts in high school, adult Monitors got paid a small amount to watch their fellow citizens, so there was never a shortage of volunteers.

The woman's eyes met Becca's. Becca quickly looked away.

She had never been afraid of Monitors before.

"There's not much to tell," Jake was saying. "Grew up here, moved away, came back with my dad after my parents split up. Suffering through school until I graduate." He shrugged. "I've lived a boring life."

"That's just what a spy would say." She matched his teasing tone before she realized she was doing it.

"I could always make something up," he offered. "Would it sound more believable if I told you I was raised by wolves for the first ten years of my life?"

"Maybe. It would depend on how convincingly you could howl." An unexpected smile creased the corners of her mouth. Even with her suspicions, something about him put her at ease. The rhythm of his voice made her mind stop racing.

Of course, if he really was a spy, he was probably doing that on purpose. Her smile dropped away.

The waitress approached, pen poised above her pad. Becca and Jake looked at each other. "Pepperoni?" asked Jake.

Becca nodded. "And... anchovies." Why make this easy for him?

Jake raised his eyebrows. "All right. Pepperoni and anchovies." He passed their order along to the waitress. When she was gone, he tilted his head at Becca. "You don't strike me as the anchovy type."

"I'm full of surprises." She smiled again without meaning to.

She wished he would quit talking to her like that, and quit looking at her like he was actually interested in her. This would be a lot easier if he'd start asking her questions about Heather instead. That way she'd know for sure.

But then he'd lose his chance to catch her off-guard, and she wouldn't tell him anything. If he wanted to find out whether Heather was a dissident, it made a lot more sense for him to do what he was doing. Make her let her guard down. Get her to like him.

Jake rested his arms on the table and leaned closer. "So what about you? If having a boring life means I'm a spy, what makes your life so interesting?"

She bit her lip and frowned in an exaggerated look of concern. "Okay. You caught me. My life is as boring as yours.

Does that make me a spy too?"

He laughed, and she smiled back. She tried to remind herself that she was only pretending to have a good time.

As they talked, Becca kept waiting for him to segue into a question about Heather. He didn't. In fact, Heather's name didn't come up once in the conversation. They talked about school, and about the town where Jake had lived for the past couple of years, and about which of them had seen the most bad movies in their lifetime. Their pizza arrived, and they paused to scarf down two slices each—the anchovies actually weren't so bad, and if they bothered Jake, he didn't show it—and then they talked some more while munching on what was left.

Sometimes Becca almost forgot the real reason Jake had brought her here.

And when Jake still didn't ask about Heather, she started to wonder if maybe he had been telling the truth after all.

Did she have any concrete reason to think he was a spy? She thought about it, but couldn't come up with anything.

And then there was what he had done when Laine had gone after Heather. Maybe he hadn't done it to make Becca less suspicious. Maybe he really had just wanted to help.

As Becca finished the final piece of pizza, Jake glanced down at his watch.

"I guess I really am that boring," said Becca lightly. "I must be working for Internal."

"What?" Jake frowned. "Oh! No, it's just my dad. He doesn't like me to be gone for too long."

"The overprotective type?" Becca's mom used to get like that, before she started spending too much time at work to be able to keep track of Becca's whereabouts. Now, out of necessity, she pretty much trusted Becca to keep herself out of trouble.

At least, she had until she had decided Heather was a dissident.

"It's not like that." Jake's whole demeanor had changed. He seemed to shrink, like he was collapsing in on himself. "When my mom died, he took it really hard. He's still having a tough time. I stay home as much as I can, to make things easier for him."

Becca opened her mouth to say something sympathetic—and stopped.

Something was wrong with what he had said.

It took her a few seconds to place it. "You said your parents split up."

Seconds stretched by. Jake didn't answer.

"You know what? Don't bother coming up with an explanation. I don't care." Becca stood up. She pushed her chair in so hard it squealed against the floor.

So he had lied to her. No big surprise there. It wasn't as if she had ever really thought he was interested in her as anything other than a source of information. Why did it make her so angry to find confirmation of what she had already known?

Jake started to say something. Becca interrupted. "I don't want to hear it. Just take me home."

* * *

When Becca came in, her mom was waiting for her. She set aside the papers in her lap as Becca closed the door behind her. "You're back early."

At the sound of her mom's voice, Becca's nausea returned. She wished she hadn't eaten all that pizza. "I'm going to bed."

Her mom's eyebrows rose. "It's not even nine o'clock." She patted the spot next to her. "How about sitting with me for a while and telling me about this guy?"

"Not now, all right? I'm really tired."

"If we're going to fix whatever went wrong between us, we have to start somewhere."

Becca's stomach churned. "I don't want to talk, okay? I just want to go to bed."

"Your best friend is a dissident. You go on dates without telling me. Something is bothering you, but you won't talk about it." Becca's mom stood up. "Something is wrong here. You know it as well as I do."

Like any of that meant anything compared to what Becca's mom had done. Something was wrong here, but it wasn't Becca's fault. "Maybe you can tell *me* something." Her voice came out harsher than she had intended. "What exactly did Heather do besides having the wrong parents?"

Her mom sighed. "I thought we were done discussing this. Dissident parents often pass their ideology on to their children. I could show you a hundred different examples—and in most of those cases, the children look completely innocent." She paused. "Is that what this is about? Heather?"

No, it's about how you lied to me. How you've been lying to everyone by giving dissidents manufactured crimes to confess to on TV before their executions. "So if you work for Internal, that must mean I work for Internal too, right?"

"It's not as simple as that, and you know it."

"If she's so obviously a dissident, why not arrest her? Why

let her go and then send spies to talk to her friends?" Becca's voice rose. "Have any of you people actually talked to her? She's the furthest thing there is from a dissident. The idea of her parents being dissidents is tearing her apart." Despite the problems they were having, Becca was more certain than ever that Heather wasn't a dissident. Heather would never have reacted the way she had to Becca's revelation otherwise.

Heather had rejected the information. Becca had tried to get her to believe it. Which of them had acted like a dissident?

Only a dissident would think any of that could be true.

She pushed the thought away. She could deal with it later. Much later.

"Wait." Her mom frowned. "What do you mean, send spies to talk to her friends?"

"That guy I went out with? Turns out he was just trying to get information about Heather." She tried to make it sound like it was no big deal. Her voice still came out angry.

Her mom's lips tightened. "And why was he trying to get this information from you? Why not from Heather?"

"How should I know? I guess he thought I'd be less likely to suspect him."

Her mom straightened her shoulders. She looked like she was preparing for battle. "This is completely inappropriate. They should have arrested that girl along with her parents. To let her go and then spy on my daughter, as though you're the criminal here... and taking you on a date to do it, no less..." She brought her focus back to Becca. "This is going to stop right now." She pulled out her phone. "What's his name?"

"Jake." Becca thought. "He never told me his last name."

Her mom dialed a number. She walked into the kitchen as she spoke. Becca couldn't make out the words, but there was no misinterpreting the tone of her voice.

And then, abruptly, her voice softened, shifted from furious to subdued.

She came back into the living room. The anger in her eyes was gone, replaced with confusion. "Since you didn't know his name, I asked about all surveillance on Heather." She hesitated.

"And?"

"There is no surveillance on Heather."

chapter seven

Jake's house was half the size of Heather's aunt's, with peeling brown paint and a half-unhinged screen door. A few dead plants lined the front walk. Becca had driven past it three times before she had finally spotted it. It was one of those places she had stopped seeing a long time ago after passing it on the ride to and from school every day.

She pulled into the driveway and winced as she hit a pothole. She slammed the car door and strode up the walk, choking on the smell of exhaust from the busy road.

Whatever game Jake was playing, Becca was going to get an explanation.

If he was home. There weren't any other cars in the driveway. She couldn't even see if there were any lights on inside the house; the curtains were pulled tight.

She had spent most of the day trying to figure out what to do about what she had found out yesterday. Then she had spent another twenty minutes convincing her mom to let her use the car, when her mom had wanted to spend her rare free evening doing some mother-daughter bonding. It had never occurred to her that Jake might not be home.

She reached out to ring the doorbell—but it had no button, just a couple of wires spilling out of the hole where the button should have been. She opened the screen door and knocked instead.

No answer.

Maybe nobody was home. Maybe she had made this trip for nothing.

Maybe it was a sign.

She could leave and spend the rest of the day at the playground avoiding her mom. She could just write Jake off as a liar and a creep, and walk in the other direction whenever she saw him at school.

No. She wasn't giving up yet. Jake owed her an explanation.

She knocked again, louder.

Still no answer—but to her right, one of the curtains twitched.

She knocked a third time, loud enough that Jake would probably think she was Enforcement. Not that Enforcement usually bothered to knock at all.

Slowly, the door swung open.

Becca opened her mouth, ready to get some answers out of Jake—and snapped it shut again when she saw a man with a tangled gray beard wearing a pair of ratty pajamas. Definitely not Jake.

They blinked at each other for a few seconds.

This man had to be Jake's dad. Becca had assumed Jake had been lying about his dad just like he had lied about his mom. Now, looking at the man in front of her, she wondered if that part had actually been true.

"Is Jake home?" Becca asked.

"I thought you were dead," the man exclaimed at the same moment.

His eyes were round; his mouth hung slightly open. He fixed his eyes on her like he was afraid she would disappear if he looked away.

Before Becca could try to figure out what he meant, he opened the door wider and motioned her inside.

Becca hung back. "I think you've got the wrong person. I'm just looking for Jake. I know him from school."

He shook his head so hard that Becca felt dizzy. "Don't lie to me. Why are you lying to me? I'd know you anywhere." He grabbed her wrist and, before she could think of resisting, pulled her inside.

She stumbled through the front door. Immediately she jerked her arm away and turned back around, but he had already slammed the door shut behind her. He stood between her and the exit, tears streaming down his face. "You were gone so long." His voice broke. "You let me think you were dead. How could you? Didn't you know how much we missed you?"

Becca tried to keep her voice level. "There's been some mistake. I'm not who you think I am." She searched the room for something she could use as a weapon if he turned violent. The room was practically bare. A tattered couch, a TV in the corner showing executions. Four neat but precariously tall stacks of unopened mail next to the door. On the wall, a picture hung the wrong way around, so that all Becca could see was the back of the frame.

That was it. Nothing Becca could use. Nothing to protect her from this lunatic.

He reached a trembling hand toward her hair, but stopped just short of touching her. "You can't be alive. You can't. I saw you die."

"I'm sorry about whatever happened," said Becca, making her speech low and soothing, trying not to let him see her fear. She didn't know what might set him off. "But whoever you're looking for... I'm not her." Could she open the window and climb out? Probably not before he caught her. "Just step away from the door and let me leave. Please."

The door burst open, catching Jake's dad in the back. He yelped and stumbled out of the way.

Jake rushed into the house, clutching two bulging bags of groceries. "Dad? What happened? Whose car is—" He saw Becca and froze. He dropped the bags to the floor, and Becca heard the crunch of breaking glass.

"What the *hell* are you doing here?" Jake roared. His voice filled the tiny room. However frightening he had sounded when he had threatened Laine, it was nothing compared to now.

Her thoughts of confrontation evaporated. "I came to ask you something, but it wasn't important. I was just leaving."

Yellow liquid seeped out of one of the grocery bags. Jake either didn't notice or didn't care. "How dare you come into my home? How dare you come near my family?"

"I wasn't... he thought..." Becca gave up on explanations. She started for the door, but Jake was still standing between her and the way out.

Jake slowly walked up to her until his toes touched hers. Abruptly, his voice dropped to a whisper. "If you ever come near my father again," he hissed, "I'll kill you."

Before Becca could react, Jake grabbed for her. He dug his fingers into her arm and propelled her out the door. She only just managed to stay on her feet.

"Get out!" he screamed as she ran for the car.

* * *

From her vantage point at the top of the slide, Becca spotted the rust-ridden death trap of a car as soon as it pulled up.

The engine shut off with a strangled growl. Becca knew who was inside before the driver's-side door opened. That was the same car that had been parked beside hers when she had left Jake's house an hour ago.

Jake walked across the playground to her. He stopped at the bottom of the slide. "I was hoping you'd be here." His smile was nowhere to be found. Instead, his face was a mess of relief and hope and fear. He looked... vulnerable. His shoulders were hunched; he walked with small, hesitant steps. A jarring contrast to his earlier fury.

"I thought you didn't ever want to see me again." She managed to keep most of the fear out of her voice.

"I'm sorry about what happened back there. I didn't mean to yell at you like that." He sounded like a different person. All his carefree confidence was gone.

He watched her like he was waiting for an answer. She didn't give him one. What was she supposed to say? *It's okay that you lied to me, tried to manipulate me, and then threatened to kill me.* That wasn't going to happen. Not without a really good reason.

Seeing him down there reminded her of the first time she had run into him at the playground. She frowned at the memory. It had taken her almost twenty minutes to get back here from Jake's house this afternoon... and yet Jake had just happened to come here the other day to think? Becca's skin prickled.

When she didn't answer, Jake motioned her down the ladder. "Come down here and we'll talk."

"I'd rather not." She crouched in a defensive position, waiting for him to climb the ladder after her.

Instead, he sat at the bottom of the rusted slide. "Why did you come to my house, anyway?"

Now that she didn't seem to be in any immediate danger, Becca's earlier anger began to boil up, overtaking her fear.

She was so sick of being lied to.

"I'm not the one who needs to explain myself. If you're not working for Internal, why did you want to know about Heather? Why did you take me on that date? Why did you lie about your mom? Who did your dad think I was?" Her voice rose with every question. "And why did you go nuts when I came to your house?"

"I told you," said Jake. Not angry like she had expected. Quiet. Defeated. "I wanted to know about Heather because I didn't think it was right the way everyone was treating her. That's it. And I took you out to dinner because I like you—is that so hard to believe? As for the rest..." He looked up at her with pleading eyes. "Can't you just forget about all that?"

Becca raised her eyebrows. "You're kidding, right?"

"I'm sorry, okay? I don't know what was wrong with me.

As soon as I realized what I had said to you..." He hunched over, curling his hands into fists. "I just want to make things right."

"If you don't want to tell me the truth, fine," said Becca. "You leave me alone and I'll leave you alone. But don't try to pretend we have some kind of relationship, and don't *ever* lie to me again."

"Please. Let's start over." He sounded like the words were choking him, like Becca's answer was a matter of life and death.

"I already gave you that chance. We're going in circles here. Tell me what's going on, or don't talk to me again."

She waited... and waited. He didn't speak. He didn't even move.

He wasn't going to answer her.

But he didn't look like he was planning on leaving, either. And Becca couldn't stay here all night.

He didn't hurt me earlier, even as angry as he was, she told herself. *He won't hurt me now.* But the hate in his voice when he had threatened Laine still echoed in her ears.

She started climbing down the ladder.

Jake didn't move as she made it to the bottom of the ladder, as she began walking toward the road. She paused and looked back at him one more time. He was still sitting a the bottom of the slide, eyes closed, fists clenched. She couldn't even tell whether he knew she had moved.

Becca wanted to scream at him, to rush up and shake him until some sort of logical explanation fell out. But no matter what Jake told her, it wouldn't be what she wanted. He could explain what he had done, but he could never explain her mother.

She kept walking.

As she reached the road, Jake called after her. "Wait."

She stopped.

"I'll tell you what you want to know."

Becca waited while Jake dragged himself across the sea of weeds. When he reached her, he opened his mouth, then closed it again. It took him a moment to get the words out.

"Three years ago, Internal arrested me and my family." It came out in a rush. "We weren't dissidents. A friend of my dad's was staying with us that year, and it turned out he was publishing a dissident newspaper. We didn't find out until it was too late." He looked at her with fear in his eyes. "We weren't dissidents," he repeated.

Most people probably wouldn't have believed his denials. But Becca's mom had told her stories most people never heard. Every once in a while, Internal made a mistake.

Of course, that was what she had kept telling herself about Heather's parents.

But her mom had kil—They had been executed. Jake and his dad were still alive. Just like Heather.

"They let you go," she said, thinking aloud. "So they must have realized they were wrong about you."

Jake nodded. "But not until... not for a while. My mom died in there."

Had they made her confess to something she hadn't done? She tried to push the thought away. "I'm sorry."

"It's over now." Jake moved his shoulders in a convulsive imitation of a shrug. "But that's why I got like that when I saw you at my house. No one ever comes there—just me and my dad. And you saw what he's like now. He's... fragile. When I saw you inside, all I could think was that someone might hurt him."

And no wonder, after what had happened to his mom. She shuddered.

"And that's why I was asking about Heather," Jake continued. "I wasn't spying for anyone. I just wanted to know how she was doing, because I know what it's like."

"So why talk to me?" Becca asked. "Why not go to her directly?"

"I didn't know if she'd want to talk to me. I figured she might just want to be left alone. Besides..." He paused. "It wasn't just about Heather. I wanted to get to know you."

Becca, still trying to process his revelation about his arrest, couldn't respond with anything but a blank stare.

"When Internal let us go, everyone knew what had happened," said Jake. "None of my friends would speak to me, except to call me a dissident. I got beaten up every day. I couldn't fight back, in case hurting them got me arrested again. They broke one of my ribs once. I was afraid one day they'd go too far and kill me." He rubbed his chest like he could still feel the pain of the broken rib. "We moved out to live with my grandparents—my mom's parents—for a while. No one at my new school knew about any of it. I kept waiting for someone to call me a dissident, or to say something about my mom, but they never found out. I almost got used to it—being normal again.

"Of course, then my grandparents decided they'd rather pay for us to move back here than keep us in their house any longer than they had to. I guess I should be grateful they kept us around as long as they did—my dad isn't exactly easy to live with. So they pay the rent and send us just enough money to live on—" A hint of bitterness crept into his voice. "—And we stay here where they don't have to deal with us."

He paused for a moment, staring at the ground. "When we came back here, I stayed as invisible as possible. I didn't want anybody to recognize me. A few people have, but it's nothing like before. But that's only because I don't let them notice me. I make sure not to be too loud, or too quiet, or too smart, or too anything."

But he hadn't been invisible when he had confronted Laine. He had risked having people notice him to help Heather.

She kept listening.

"I saw it happen all over again with Heather. But you didn't turn on her, even after people started calling you a dissident too. I thought..." He laughed a little. "It sounds pathetic. I thought with you maybe I wouldn't have to be invisible."

What could Becca say to all that?

"I had no idea." She shook her head. "I thought you were using me somehow—either to get information about Heather for Internal, or... I didn't even know what." She paused. "I'm sorry."

"How were you supposed to know?" He stood awkwardly, hands jammed into his pockets. "So... can we start over?" His smile was so slight, Becca almost didn't see it. "Again?"

By telling her what had happened to him, he had risked her turning against him like everybody else. He had poured his heart out to her. How could she turn him away after that?

She smiled back. A peace offering. "Of course we can."

* * *

Becca's head was still full of her conversation with Jake when she scanned the cafeteria for Heather the next Monday.

She almost didn't recognize her. Heather wasn't wearing any makeup, and her hair stuck out in tangled curls. She moved without grace; as Becca watched, she stumbled to an empty table in the corner and set her tray down so hard a drop of chili jumped up onto her shirt. She didn't seem to notice.

Becca crossed the room and slid her tray into the space across from Heather.

"Whoever you are, just leave me alone," Heather muttered. She looked up. "Oh," she said flatly. "It's you."

Becca sat down. "I've been looking for you all morning. I thought maybe you had skipped school again."

Heather studied her chili as though it were an alien lifeform. "What do you want?" For a second Becca wasn't sure whether Heather was talking to her or the chili.

Becca took a deep breath. "I'm sorry."

She'd had all day Sunday to think about her conversation with Heather, and about what Jake had told her. And the more she thought, the more she knew she had been wrong to push Heather about what she had found in her mom's files. Heather didn't need that kind of pressure right now. She didn't need that reminder of what her parents had been.

That would leave Becca with nobody to talk to about what she had found. But that didn't matter right now. Heather needed a friend—Becca's conversation with Jake had shown her just how much—and she had nobody else.

"I'm sorry about... everything I said," Becca continued. She couldn't get more specific than that. Not here. "I won't talk to you about it anymore, if you don't want."

Heather stirred her chili. She didn't answer.

"Whatever you need, I'm here for you," Becca promised.

Heather spoke without looking at Becca. "I need you to leave me alone."

Becca flinched at the coldness in Heather's voice. "I should have told you about your parents sooner, too. I won't keep things from you anymore."

Heather jumped up from her chair. She slammed her hands down on the table; both their trays shook. "I said leave me alone!"

In the sudden quiet, Becca felt everyone's eyes on her.

Heather's breath came raggedly. Her eyes looked like a trapped animal's. "Please," she mumbled. "Please. Please go away."

Becca's best friend was in there somewhere. But Becca couldn't see her.

Heather didn't move. Neither did Becca.

Slowly, the conversation in the cafeteria started up again.

Heather was slipping away. Somebody had to keep her here. Keep her sane.

But hadn't Becca said she would give Heather whatever she needed?

I need you to leave me alone.

She had thought she had known what was best for Heather before, when she had put off telling her about her parents and led her to the note. It hadn't helped. If anything, she had only made things worse.

If she pushed Heather now, would she be making the same mistake all over again?

Becca swallowed her next round of apologies and walked away.

chapter eight

A knock on Becca's door dragged her out of her dream.

She muttered something incoherent and pulled her blanket up over her head. The knock came again; the blanket did nothing to muffle it.

With a sign, Becca pushed the blanket away and flicked on her light. She sat up, rubbing her eyes. "What is it?" she mumbled.

"Can I come in?" her mom asked from the other side of the door.

As if Becca could say no. "I didn't know you were home."

"I didn't have anything urgent to deal with, so I decided to come home and catch up on some sleep." The door opened, and her mom stepped inside. "Speaking of which, you're in bed early. Especially for a Saturday."

Sleeping was easier than being awake, these days. Less opportunity to think about all the things she was trying to push to the back of her mind. "I was tired."

Her mom held something out to her. Her eyes still blurry from sleep, Becca squinted at the object in her mom's hand. Her phone. She must have left it in the living room when she had gone to bed.

"Somebody called for you." Her mom crossed the room to her.

Becca reached for the phone, but her mom pulled it back. She sat down on the bed next to Becca. "Your phone said it was Jake. Is this the same Jake you thought was working for Surveillance? You told me he had stopped bothering you."

She had told the truth... sort of. In the three weeks since their conversation at the playground, they had taken the first shaky steps toward getting to know each other. They never talked about Jake's past—he never brought it up, and Becca didn't want to push him. Instead they stuck to other things, safer things, like school and TV and all the everyday inanities people talked about to fill up time. They talked almost every day... but he never bothered her.

Somehow Becca didn't think that was what her mom meant.

She straightened, trying to will herself awake. "How should I know why he called?"

"I checked your phone. You two have been talking a lot over the past couple of weeks."

Becca stopped mid-yawn. "Wait. You read my texts?"

"You told me you thought Jake was working for Surveillance. There has to be a reason you were suspicious of him."

"I was wrong about him. You had no right to go through my phone."

Her mom looked down at the phone and pursed her lips. "You haven't given me much reason to trust your judgment when it comes to friends lately."

"You mean Heather," Becca said flatly. She could always tell her mom the truth—that she and Heather hadn't spoken in almost three weeks—but no matter how things were between her and Heather, she needed her mom to know that she still stood by her friend, that she didn't believe Heather was a dissident.

"Yes. I mean Heather." Her mom shifted on the bed so she could look directly at Becca. "And now this Jake. Three weeks ago, you were sure he had ulterior motives. Now you two are... friends? More than friends?"

Becca wasn't sure what they were. For now, it didn't matter. She was someone who knew his history but wouldn't call him a dissident, the only person who hadn't started whispering behind his back after he had broken his invisibility rule by stepping in to help Heather. He was someone who was willing to talk to her, who could make her forget about Heather and her mother for moments at a time. They would figure out the rest as they went along. "We're... talking."

"And whatever made you suspicious of him doesn't matter anymore?"

Her mom didn't even accept her friendship with Heather. What would she think of Jake, if she knew Internal had arrested him? If her mom was willing to condemn Heather based on what her parents had done, Becca doubted it would matter that Internal had realized their mistake and let Jake go.

Becca tried to force her half-asleep brain to think. "I guess I got paranoid after what happened with Heather. It seemed strange for him to ask me out when everyone else was treating me like a disease. So when he asked me about Heather, I assumed that had to be the reason."

"I can't control who you spend your time with," said her mom. "But if you're going to keep talking to this person, I want to meet him. You should invite him over for dinner sometime."

Becca started shaking her head before her mom had even finished her sentence. "I told you I was wrong about him. I'm not allowed to be wrong about somebody?"

"I'm not saying you couldn't have been wrong about him before. I'm concerned that you might be wrong about him now."

"You used to trust my judgment." That wasn't the real problem, though. For the first time in her life, she didn't care what her mom thought of her. But after what Jake had gone through, how could she bring him here to eat across the table from the one person who most represented Processing?

"That was before you insisted on maintaining a friendship with the daughter of two dissidents."

If Heather is a dissident because of her parents, what does being your daughter make me? "You said yourself, you can't control who I spend time with."

"That doesn't mean I won't do what I can to protect you." Her mom sat a little straighter. "You can let me meet him, or I can have Investigation look into him."

Becca's mouth fell open. "Because you think anyone I'm friends with must be a dissident?"

"Because he was asking you suspicious questions about the daughter of confirmed dissidents. Your suspicions, whether or not you still have them, are more than enough for Internal to take an interest."

Becca felt sick. Had her mom been like this all along? How had she never noticed? "So if I don't let you meet him, you'll report him as a dissident for something I said when I didn't even know him?"

"Of course not!" Her mom looked scandalized, and vaguely disgusted. "You think I would compromise my integrity by reporting him as a dissident, with practically nothing to support that accusation, because I was worried about his relationship with you?" She shook her head. "I would have Surveillance look into it and find out whether there's any reason to suspect dissident activity. That's all."

Was that the same integrity that let her get false confessions out of dissidents and make Anna disappear? Becca swallowed the retort. She should be grateful her mom wasn't willing to report Jake for no good reason.

But if her mom had Surveillance investigate him, they would find out about the arrest. After that, at best she would find some way to keep Becca away from him, no matter what she said about not being able to control who Becca spent her time with. At worst, she would take that as all the proof she needed, and Jake would disappear like Anna.

"I'll invite him over for dinner," said Becca, already planning how to put it off.

"Soon," her mom said, as if she could see what Becca was thinking.

"Soon," Becca agreed.

Her mom didn't get up. "I have to go in to work tomorrow morning, but I'll be home in plenty of time for dinner."

Becca sighed loud enough for her mom to hear. "I'll see if

he can make it."

* * *

"So, Jake," said Becca's mom. "Tell me about yourself."

Jake sat in the extra chair Becca's mom had squeezed into the kitchen, his long legs spilling out from under the table. To his left, Becca watched him warily. He didn't know about her mom's threat, so he might not know how careful he had to be. And he was bound to show some hint of stress that her mom would misinterpret. Her mom's reputation made people nervous under the best of circumstances. Even when they hadn't spent time in Processing. Even when they didn't have parents who had died there.

Jake shrugged like he had when Becca had asked him that question, but this time it looked jerky and uncoordinated. "There's not much to tell."

Come on, Jake. Give her something. Give her some reason to trust you.

She had told Jake he didn't have to do this. She hadn't told him what her mom had threatened to do if he didn't; the lie of omission had given her a twinge of guilt, but she hadn't wanted him to think he was in danger of being arrested again. She hadn't figured out what she would tell him if he didn't agree to come, but that turned out not to be an issue—he had agreed after only a slight hesitation.

Now she wondered if she should have told him the whole truth after all. Maybe then he'd know what was at stake.

He's not a dissident, she reminded herself. *He's not like Heather's parents. Even if she does have him investigated, the worst that can happen is that she'll find out about the arrest and try to stop me from seeing him. They won't arrest him again.*

Unless the rest of Internal cared as little about the truth as her mom did.

"The lasagna came out great," said Becca, a little too loudly. "Thanks, Mom." She forced another forkful into her mouth. Normally she loved her mom's lasagna, but tonight even the thought of eating made her stomach rebel. Just being at the same table with her mom did that to her lately.

"I'm glad you like it." Her mom gave Becca a brief smile before returning her attention to Jake. "I'm out of practice. I don't get much time to cook anymore. Some days I'm lucky if I make it home from work before midnight."

Don't start talking about work, Becca prayed.

"But you don't want to hear about dissidents over dinner," said her mom. She eyed Jake, a quizzical frown creasing her forehead. "Becca said you two have only known each other a couple of weeks."

Jake nodded. "We just moved back here two months ago." He darted his eyes around the kitchen—searching for an escape route, maybe. He looked everywhere but at Becca's mom. Becca cringed inwardly. *This would be a great time for you to act invisible.*

The less he looked at her mom, the more closely her mom watched him. "But you used to live around here? Did you two know each other back then?"

Becca dropped her fork onto her plate. "Mom, why are you asking this stuff? I told you, we just met a couple of weeks ago. Why does it matter, anyway?" As if Jake weren't having a hard enough time acting normal.

Her mom didn't even acknowledge her. Her frown deepened. "Do I know your parents, then?"

Jake stabbed at his lasagna. "I don't think so. Neither of them ever worked for Internal."

Becca searched for something she could say to turn the conversation in a better direction—the last thing Jake needed was a reminder of his parents. She came up blank.

"Are you sure?" her mom pressed.

"I'm sure." Jake was methodically dismantling his lasagna now. He spread it layer by layer across his plate.

Above the stove, the clock ticked away the seconds. How many more before this meal was over?

Her mom leaned a little closer to Jake, studying his face. "I could have sworn I—" She drew back. Her chair clattered to the floor behind her as she jerked up out of her seat.

She grabbed Jake's arm and yanked him out of his chair. "Get out." Her words sliced through the air. "Get out of my kitchen. Get out of my apartment. And don't you *ever* come near my daughter again."

Becca stood up, knowing she had to intervene but not sure how. What was her mom doing? What had she seen in Jake to cause this kind of reaction? First the weird questions, and now—

She went cold as the truth hit her.

Jake swayed on his feet, looking from Becca's mom to the doorway and back again. "I—"

"Get out," her mom repeated, in a whisper more dangerous than a roar. "Don't say another word. Just leave this apartment right now."

Becca had to do something. Say something to Jake, or to her mom, or...

She stayed where she was, still and silent, as Jake backed out of the kitchen.

* * *

As soon as the apartment door closed, Becca's mom sagged against the counter. "Please tell me you didn't know."

Becca stayed where she was. She couldn't move. "You killed her, didn't you? You killed Jake's mother."

Her mom let out a long, ragged breath. "You knew. You knew about him and his family, and you still…" She clutched the counter like she was afraid she might fall. "I don't know you anymore."

I don't know you anymore. Heather had said the same thing.

"She wasn't a dissident. She was innocent. They all were." Becca stumbled back and dropped, half-falling, into her chair. "Did you know? Did you even care?"

"That's what he told you? And you believed him?" Her mom laughed without humor. "You should have known better than to expect the truth from a dissident."

"He told me about his dad's friend." Becca traced the fake wood grains on the plastic-topped table, in the space beside her mostly-full plate of lasagna. She couldn't look at her mom. If she did, she would have to try to figure out whether she was looking at the woman who had raised her or the stranger who had killed Jake's mother.

"What friend?" Her mom sounded like she really didn't know what Becca was talking about. Becca knew better. She knew how well her mom could lie.

"The dissident. The reason Jake and his family were arrested." Becca scraped her fingernail along the pattern she was tracing, trying to scratch a line. "Don't pretend you don't know."

Her mom sat down in Jake's chair. She scraped the lasagna off her own plate and stacked Jake's on top of it. "Becca... I have no idea what you're talking about. I don't know what kind of lies he told you, but that's all they were. Lies."

Becca turned her face away, toward the wall. "How do I know you're not the one lying?" She didn't realize how close she was to tears until she heard her voice waver.

She felt her mom pull back. "You'd trust a dissident's word over mine?"

"It's not like you haven't lied to me before." If she focused hard enough on the wall, maybe her mom's voice would disappear. Maybe it would all disappear.

"When?" her mom demanded. "When have I lied to you?"

Why didn't she just tell her mom what she had found in those files? Why had she avoided the subject for so long? Did she really think her own mother would report her?

Tell her. Nothing will happen. Just say it.

She didn't say it.

"If Jake and his family were dissidents, why did you let him and his dad go?" she asked instead.

Her mom sighed. "Turn around and look at me. This is ridiculous."

Reluctantly, Becca turned away from the wall and met her mom's eyes. She had expected to see anger there. Instead, her mom looked... scared. No. Terrified.

"Letting them go wasn't my choice," her mom said. "The people who make these decisions always have complex reasons, usually involving the benefits of strengthening Internal's presence in society by releasing the occasional prisoner who has reason to fear us. If it were up to me, it would never happen." She sighed again. "They said, the way they always do in these situations, that Jake and his father posed no further threat to society. They don't understand that no dissident is harmless." She paused. "But even assuming they were right, harmless and innocent are not the same thing. There was never any question that Jake and his family were dissidents."

What if her mom was telling the truth? What if Jake really was a dissident?

But why should Becca believe a word her mom said?

"Do you want me to tell you the truth about why he was arrested?" her mom asked.

Becca didn't answer.

Her mom started talking anyway. "His family was publishing a dissident newspaper from their house. He and his parents were only peripherally involved; his older sister was the main problem."

"He told me about the newspaper," Becca interrupted. "None of them had anything to do with it. It was their dad's friend." But her mom's words had sparked a flicker of doubt in her mind. Jake had never mentioned a sister. She thought back to how Jake's dad had reacted to her. When he had looked at her, had he seen a lost daughter?

If Jake's sister was real... what had happened to her?

"His sister was connected with a minor dissident group. Public Relations appropriated her for televised execution before we could get any names from her, but she herself admitted the connection." Her mom took hold of Becca's chin and made Becca look her in the eye. "They were not innocent."

If this was true, why would Jake have told her about the arrest in the first place? Why wouldn't he have avoided the subject entirely, instead of telling her a half-truth that might drive her away?

Her mom let go. "His sister was executed," she finished. "His mother died under interrogation. He and his father were released, against my wishes."

"What did you want to do with them?" Becca snapped. "Did you want to kill them too?"

She imagined Jake as he must have been after his release. Sent back into the world as if nothing had happened, as if nothing were different. His mother dead, and, if her mom was telling the truth, his older sister too. His father... changed. Day after day of getting beaten up at school, then going home to a half-empty house and trying to take care of his dad. How had he survived?

Her mom pushed the plates aside, stopping just short of sending them crashing to the floor. "I don't know what's happening to you, Becca, but it's scaring me. I could understand your loyalty to Heather; you've been friends with her for years. But then you defended that other dissident—Anna—after that rumor she passed on to you. And now..." She studied Becca's face as carefully as she had Jake's a few minutes ago. Whatever answers she found there didn't diminish the fear in her eyes. "Now you're defending a dissident. Do you understand what you're saying when you tell me you believe his story over mine? Do you understand what it means for you to imply that it would have been wrong to kill them? Do you?"

Becca couldn't think about what her mom was saying. About what it meant. Better to focus on what her mom had done. She let the anger fill her, a shield against her mom's implied accusations.

"So you do wish you had killed him. How old was he then? Thirteen? And you would have shot him along with his sister." As she spoke, her mom's features rearranged, became unfamiliar. Her mom had said she didn't know Becca anymore, but she was the one who had changed.

No. This was who she had always been. Becca had just been too blind to see it.

"I should have gone with Dad when he left," Becca spat. "Maybe he had the right idea. Maybe he knew the truth about you all along."

The words hung in the air between them.

They both jumped as the kitchen phone rang.

Becca's mom got up first. She picked the phone up from the counter. "Hello?" She listened for a moment, then handed the phone to Becca, her face expressionless. "It's for you."

Only one person called Becca on the land line instead of her cell phone.

Becca checked the date on her watch. The first Sunday of the month. She had forgotten.

Becca took the phone from her mom. "Hi, Dad."

chapter nine

Becca sat on her bed with her legs tucked under her, cradling the phone against her ear. Somewhere on the other side of the door, her mom was probably still thinking about what she had said. Becca hadn't meant to say it. The words had slipped out before she was fully aware of them. Had she crossed a line? Said something unforgivable?

Why did it matter? Why did she care whether she hurt her mom, after everything her mom had done?

Her dad had asked her something. "Sorry, I didn't hear you."

"How's school going?" her dad repeated in his soft voice.

She answered on autopilot. "Fine, I guess." Now that she wasn't in the same room as her mom, it was harder to keep her anger fresh. She couldn't renew it by looking at her mom and seeing how the person she thought she knew had actually been somebody else all along. The rest of the conversation, the part she had been trying not to think about, began to creep back into her mind.

Do you understand what you're saying when you tell me you believe his story over mine? Do you understand what it means for you to imply it would have been wrong to kill them?

"Becca? Are you still there?"

"I'm still here." Becca tried to focus on her dad's voice, tried to let it block out the echoes of other voices.

Only a dissident would think any of that could be true.

But she had found proof. That changed everything, didn't it? How could she not believe, now that she had proof?

Did it still make her a dissident?

Did being glad Jake was alive make her a dissident? Did being angry that her mom had killed his mom?

Dissident. The word echoed through her mind.

Her dad was talking again. Becca tried to concentrate, but he sounded like he was speaking some alien language. He paused. Was he waiting for an answer? What had he asked her?

"Are you okay?" The words came through clearly this time. From the way he said it, she guessed it wasn't the first time he had asked the question.

"I'm fine," she said, but winced as her answer came out too fast, too clipped. She struggled to come up with a better response, but her mind dragged her back down.

Dissident.

Becca knew what dissidents were. They were the people Internal arrested every day, the people trying to poison society against the government so they could bring back the old corrupt system. Becca's mom had raised her to believe in the importance of a safe and stable world, a world ruled by justice. Whatever she might think of her mom now, Becca still believed in that world. She didn't want any part of the world the dissidents were trying to create—so how could she be a dissident?

But how much of what she knew about the dissidents was true, and how much had been manufactured by people like her mom?

Back to her mom again. Back where she had started.

She tried to build her anger up again, tried to remind herself of all the things her mom had done. All the ways she had lied. But instead of boiling over, the anger sat in her belly like a piece of bad meat. Maybe her mom hadn't betrayed her after all. Maybe Becca was the traitor here. *Dissident.*

"If you don't want to talk about it, that's okay," her dad was saying. "But if there's any way I can help..."

Her dad's words barely penetrated her thoughts—but the sound of his voice sparked a memory, one she clung to like a lifeline. He didn't like her mom's job either, or a lot of the things Internal did. It was the reason he had left. Becca could still remember the arguments.

If he could have doubts about Internal without being a dissident, so could she.

She tried to lighten her voice, tried to make it sound like this wasn't a big deal. "Can I ask you something?"

"Shoot."

She tried to figure out how to word her question without sounding like she was making accusations. "What made you hate Mom's job enough to leave?"

His answer, when it came, was sharp. "What has your mother been telling you?"

"What? This isn't about her. I——"

"I never had a problem with her job," her dad insisted. "No matter what she says."

Becca frowned. "But… I remember. I used to hear you arguing about it." The memories, blurry from years of disuse, sharpened as she called them to mind again. A fight in the middle of the night. *All she said was that her life wasn't that bad under the old regime. How is that enough to condemn her to death?* Another, hastily interrupted as Becca came in from the yard. *I know the kinds of things you do in that place. How can I watch you hug Becca and not think about the blood on your hands?*

"I always supported your mother." Her dad interrupted the memories. Becca recognized the tension in his voice. She could hear it in her own thoughts.

Did he hear the word echoing in his head too?

Dissident.

In his denials, she could hear herself thirty years from now, insisting that she had never doubted any dissidents' confessions. Pushing the evidence she had found to the back of her mind because the only alternative was to become the enemy.

Lying like everybody else did. Like her dad was right now.

Why couldn't anyone just tell her the truth?

"If you didn't have a problem with her job," she challenged him, "then why did you two argue about it all the time?"

"You were a kid. You misunderstood."

Maybe she should let him have his denial.

And then what? If he couldn't admit his doubts, what was she supposed to do with hers? How was she supposed to quiet the accusing voice?

Her voice hardened. "I know what I heard."

Her dad waited a moment to answer. "Her job brought certain dangers with it. Things I didn't know if I could live with."

"What do you mean?" She wanted to know how he was rationalizing this to himself.

"Well, you remember what happened with your mom's friend."

Becca tried to figure out what he was talking about, but nothing came to mind. Had anything actually happened, or was he just making this up to cover over the doubts he didn't want to admit he had?

"What happened?" she asked.

"You don't remember?" He sounded surprised. "I guess you were pretty young at the time." He paused. "Internal took her husband. She blamed your mother for it. Your mother tried to help her at first, but she wouldn't listen."

Despite herself, Becca almost felt sorry for her mother. A friend who had lost family to Internal, who turned on her and pushed her away even though she'd had nothing to do with it... Becca knew all too well what that felt like. She kept waiting for Heather to call her or at least say hi at school, but when they passed each other in the halls, Heather's eyes slid over her as if she didn't exist.

She forced her attention back to her dad. "What does this have to do with why you hated Mom's job?"

Her dad hesitated. "Her friend tried to kill her."

It took Becca a moment to recover her voice. "She *what*? Why?"

"Maybe she was a dissident. Maybe losing her husband just made her snap. When your mother left work, her friend was waiting for her. Your mother barely got away in time."

Maybe her dad was making this up. But Becca didn't think so. She had a faint memory of police cars in front of the house, of the feeling that something important and scary had happened.

If her mom's friend could do something like that...

No. Heather could never kill anyone.

But the Heather she saw in the halls these days, the one who had screamed at her in the cafeteria the last time they had talked, wasn't the same Heather she used to know. Heather hadn't been that person since the night she had called Becca from 117.

Her dad was still talking, still trying to convince her he had never had any doubts. "That's why I didn't like her job. I didn't think I could live with that kind of danger. It had nothing to do with... anything else."

But Becca wasn't listening anymore.

* * *

Becca rushed into the cafeteria, out of breath. As soon as she stepped inside, she scanned the tables for Heather. She didn't see her.

She stood just inside the doors, studying the faces of everyone who walked in. She flinched at the hostile glares some of them directed at her. While the rumors about her and Heather had died down, they still weren't entirely gone. She wanted to go sit at a table in the corner and pretend she was invisible... but she had to find Heather.

Five minutes went by, then ten. Still no Heather. Was she eating someplace else? Maybe she had decided not to come to school at all.

When Heather finally walked through the doors, Becca almost didn't recognize her. She was still going without makeup, and her hair was pulled back in a plain ponytail. Her jeans and t-shirt looked more likely to have come from Becca's wardrobe than her own.

But the biggest difference was in the way she held herself. She didn't shuffle her feet and hunch her shoulders the way she had the last time Becca had seen her; she walked with her old confidence. No, *more* than her old confidence—this was something new.

Heather saw her, Becca could tell. Their eyes met for a fraction of a second before Heather looked away.

Becca blocked her path. "We need to talk."

Heather tried to walk around her. "Not right now, okay? We can talk later."

And how long would that be? Another three weeks? A month? By then it could be too late.

No, she told herself again. *Heather isn't capable of something like that.*

But if she was wrong...

She matched her steps to Heather's, keeping her body in front of her. "No. We need to talk now."

They stood like that for a moment as people shoved past them. What would Becca do if Heather said no? She had no way to force Heather to talk to her.

At last, Heather nodded. "There's a table over there." She pointed to the far corner of the room.

Becca shook her head. "Not here. Someplace quieter." *Someplace where people won't overhear.*

They left the cafeteria. On their way down the hall, they passed two of Heather's old friends headed in the opposite direction. As the girls saw Heather, one of them leaned in toward the other and whispered something. Heather didn't even look at them.

Becca ducked into their Citizenship classroom, which was empty this time of day. She was afraid Heather would just keep going, but Heather followed her into the room. Becca closed the door behind them. This was as safe as they were going to get. At least she could be relatively sure the classrooms weren't bugged. Surveillance didn't need to spend hours listening in on every class, when Monitors were more efficient and didn't cost anything.

Becca and Heather sat at a couple of empty desks near the center of the room. The shiny desks at this school still unnerved Becca a little. She missed the scuffed and scratched-up desks of the old school. They had felt lived-in. These—and everything else in this school—looked like props from a movie.

"What did you want to talk about?" The grief and uncertainty had disappeared from Heather's voice. She didn't sound like the same person Becca had talked to in the cafeteria three weeks ago. But she didn't sound like her old self, either.

Becca studied the smudged blackboard as though the right words might appear there. All she saw was a list of the ten characteristics of a good citizen, which she had memorized back in elementary school. "If you still don't want anything to do with me, that's fine. I can leave you alone after this. But I need to know something." She stopped, unwilling to even hint at the suspicion that could drive Heather out of her life for good.

Heather waited, so still and quiet that Becca wanted to ask

her what she had done with the real Heather.

At least she was looking at Becca now, and listening to her, instead of pretending she didn't exist. So what if she was acting a little strange. She was still trying to deal with losing her family, her friends, her life. Of course she wasn't back to normal yet.

"What do you need to know?" Heather asked.

"Do you blame my mom for what happened with your parents?"

"Of course not. She did what she had to do."

Heather's answer had come too easily. Like she had practiced it. Maybe Becca's suspicions hadn't been unfounded after all. Cold began creeping up her limbs.

"If you're thinking of... doing anything... don't." Becca stumbled over the words. "You'd get caught. You'd end up being executed like your parents. Anyway, my mom isn't responsible for what happened."

Heather frowned. "You're not making any sense."

What had Becca expected to accomplish by doing this? If Heather wasn't planning on trying to get revenge against her mom, the idea that Becca would suspect her of such a thing might damage their relationship beyond repair. And if she was, could Becca really talk her out of it?

But as long as the possibility existed, Becca had to do something. No matter what Becca thought of her mom, she couldn't stand back and let her die.

"You think I would, what, turn into a dissident?" Heather's voice rose. A little of her old self crept back into her face. "You were the one person in this school who didn't suspect me. I should have known you'd end up taking their side sooner or later."

"That's not what I meant. I meant if you were planning on... getting revenge against her somehow."

Heather looked at her in horror. "Against your mom? For executing a couple of dissidents? You really think I would do something like that? What's wrong with you?"

Becca felt like an idiot. The strangeness she had seen in Heather, her too-quick response to Becca's questions about her mom—they seemed like nothing when put up against the fact that she was all but accusing her best friend of... dissident activity, she realized. She had said she would never suspect Heather of being a dissident, but by bringing up a possibility like this, that was exactly what she was doing.

But still, doubts lingered in her mind.

Heather had said "for executing a couple of dissidents." Not "my parents."

Was she trying too hard to sound innocent?

Heather's chair screeched against the tile as she stood up. She walked to the window.

"I'm sorry." Becca got up to join her. "Dad told me this story about a friend of my mom's who tried to kill her after Internal took her husband. It made me kind of paranoid, I guess."

Heather didn't look at her.

"It didn't even occur to me that that would make you a dissident. I just remembered what it did to you when Internal took them, and how mad you got at me for no reason..."

Heather dug her fingernails into her palms. She drew her shoulders up and dropped her head, like a turtle trying to retreat into its shell.

Then, abruptly, her fists unclenched. Her shoulders dropped.

She turned to face Becca. "I'm sorry."

Becca blinked. If anything, she had expected Heather to demand an apology from her, not the other way around. "For what?"

"You're right. I was acting suspicious." She fiddled with something on her shirt. "You believed me when nobody else would, and I screamed at you and pushed you away. You didn't deserve that." She dropped her hands to her sides. "I had to work through a bunch of stuff in my head, and every time I saw you it reminded me of all the things I didn't want to think about."

Like how Becca felt every time she looked at her mom. The thought of being to Heather what her mom was to her made her skin crawl. She tried to shake off the feeling. "It's okay."

Heather shook her head. "It's not. You were completely justified to suspect me of... whatever. I wasn't acting like myself."

She still wasn't acting like herself. Something about the way she spoke was... wrong. It didn't sound like Heather.

Heather took a step forward.

The pin at her shoulder glittered in the light.

It took Becca a few seconds to understand what she was seeing. "You joined the Monitors."

Heather fingered the pin. "A couple of days ago."

"How could you do that, after everything that's happened?"

"They didn't want to let me in at first," said Heather. "But I explained how much I wanted to make up for what my parents were. They're going to have to watch me extra-carefully, to make sure I'm not trying to infiltrate them so I can pass information to dissidents, but that's okay. They'll start to trust me eventually."

Becca couldn't take her eyes off the pin. "That's not what I meant. How could you join them after what happened to your parents? After what we found in the photo album?"

Heather's eyes went cold. "My parents were *dissidents,* Becca."

The classroom door opened.

They both swiveled their heads toward the sound. Mr. Adams, their Citizenship teacher, stood in the doorway. "Are you supposed to be in here?" he asked. A rhetorical question.

"We were just leaving." Heather strode to the door and disappeared into the hall.

Becca had no choice but to do the same.

* * *

When Becca rang Heather's doorbell that evening, she half-expected Heather to slam the door in her face. Instead Heather met Becca's eyes with a blank expression. "Hi, Becca."

Becca looked away. Seeing a stranger looking out of Heather's eyes was too unnerving. "I, um… I was hoping we could talk."

Without a word, Heather opened the door and motioned Becca inside. Becca only caught a glimpse of the immaculate living room, with furniture in various shades of cream, before Heather led her upstairs to her room.

Heather still hadn't unpacked her things. A couple of cardboard boxes stood against the far wall, next to her bed. The room, aside from the bed and the boxes, was bare.

Becca had felt almost as comfortable in Heather's old bedroom as she did in her own. Here, she felt like an intruder.

Maybe she shouldn't have come.

But she had to find out what was going on.

Heather sat gingerly on the edge of her bed. "What did you want to talk about?" she asked, her expression bland. She sounded like she was talking to a stranger. Not her best friend of ten years.

Becca stayed standing. "What do you think? That." She gestured toward Heather's Monitor pin.

"The Monitors? What about them?" She shrugged. "I know I didn't want to join before, but you remember what I was like before. All I cared about was how much fun I was having and what other people were saying about me. Sometimes your life has to fall apart before you can really see what's important, you know?" She smiled—the first smile Becca had seen from her since her parents' arrest. It hung on her face like a badly-fitting mask.

"If you're just doing this so people will stop thinking you're a dissident, you can tell me. You don't have to pretend with me." Becca hoped that was the reason. If all this was an act, it would explain why Heather didn't seem like herself anymore. And why she would join the Monitors even after everything that had happened.

The smile dropped from Heather's face. "So you think if I actually care about something bigger than myself, I must be pretending?"

Either Heather didn't trust Becca at all anymore, or... she meant it. She believed in the Monitors, in Internal, in all of it. Not in the offhand way she used to—the way Becca used to—but the way the political kids did, the ones who had dreamed of working for Internal since kindergarten, the ones Heather and her friends had always made fun of.

"But what about your parents? What about…" The eye on Heather's pin watched her. She hesitated. Should she really be talking about this with a Monitor, of all people?

What was wrong with her? This was Heather. Her best friend. The idea of Heather trying to get revenge against her mom had almost made sense—she could see Heather going after her mom in a storm of grief, not thinking about what she was doing or what it meant. Turning Becca in, though, would take a level of coldness that Heather didn't have.

At least, the old Heather hadn't.

Becca forced herself to finish. She wouldn't let herself think something like that about her best friend. Bad enough that she had suspected her of plotting revenge. "What about the note, and the stuff I found in my mom's—"

"You said you weren't going to talk about this anymore," Heather interrupted. She crossed her arms.

"I didn't figure you wanted to hear about it yet, on top of everything else you were dealing with. But I can't forget what I found. I don't understand how you can just dismiss it."

"My parents were dissidents." Heather spoke each word with contemptuous precision. "Everything in that note was a dissident lie."

"If it was all a lie, then why did I find that file on my mom's computer that said…" She glanced down at Heather's pin again. "…that said Public Relations had told her what to get that dissident to say?"

"Maybe you misread it. Maybe someone knew you'd look there and planted it for you to find. How should I know?" She drew her arms in closer to her chest. "But you know what? I don't care. I don't care why you found whatever you found, and I don't care why my parents wrote that note in the first place. They were dissidents, and now they're gone. That's all that matters."

She sounded like she was talking about people she had seen on the news or something. Not her own parents. Becca studied Heather, looking for some trace of the grief she had seen the night she had gone to 117 to save her. She couldn't find anything.

"Why are you staring at me like that?" Heather snapped.

"They were your parents. How can you talk like they don't even matter to you?" For once she wanted what she was hearing to be a lie.

Heather looked at her in disbelief. "I thought you were the one who couldn't forget what we found. Don't you remember the stuff that note said?" Her voice rose until she was almost yelling. "They were dissidents!"

"They were your parents!"

"I wish I had never known them!" Heather propelled herself off the bed. "They pretended to be normal parents, they pretended to love me, when all along they only cared about poisoning society with their lies. They even managed to poison you! Look at what this is doing to you!"

Becca shrank back from Heather's rage. "What I found is real. Come to my apartment and I can show you." But she knew Heather wouldn't do it. Heather was turning into somebody Becca didn't know, and Becca didn't know how to stop it.

Or was Becca the one who was changing?

Dissident.

No. She wasn't the one in the wrong here. Heather didn't care about her parents anymore. She didn't care about the truth. She had pushed Becca away for no reason, and now she wouldn't listen.

Becca fed the anger, just like she had with her mom yesterday. The hotter it burned, the less the word echoed in her mind.

"First my parents. Now you." Heather sagged back onto the bed, like her legs wouldn't hold her anymore. A second ago she had sounded ready to explode; now her voice quavered with the threat of tears. "Are you turning into a dissident now? Is that what this is?"

The echoes got louder, roaring in Becca's ears, only now they spoke with Heather's voice. *Dissident.*

"I'm not a dissident," she whispered.

It felt like a lie.

"Then why are you doing this? Why can't you just leave it alone?" Heather swiped the back of her hand across her eyes. "Like it's not hard enough knowing what my parents were without you acting like you're on their side."

On their side.

A dissident.

She tried to focus the anger, bring it closer, build it hotter. She tried to remember that Heather was the one who was wrong.

It was getting harder. Harder to remember that she wasn't a dissident. Harder to make herself believe it.

"What about what you're doing?" She flung the words at Heather. "Your parents have only been dead a few weeks, and you're throwing them away like they never mattered."

Heather didn't answer. Her shoulders curled; she started trembling. It took Becca a minute to realize she was crying.

Becca wanted to apologize... but if she did, it would mean she was wrong and Heather was right. And if Heather was right, that meant Becca was what Heather said she was.

Finally, Heather looked up, her face streaked with tears. All the missing grief had come back again, all at once. "I can't let myself forget that they were dissidents," she whispered. "Not ever. If I do, I'll start hating Internal for killing them. And then I'll end up just like them."

Becca's anger drained away, leaving only the echoes. *Dissident. Dissident.*

Heather wiped away her tears. The emotion vanished from her face so quickly Becca wondered if she had imagined it. "Are you done talking like a dissident?"

As though nothing had happened. As though she had never started crying.

"Actually," said Becca, "I should probably go." She had to get out of here. Away from this person who looked like her best friend but wasn't. Away from the word that got louder in her head every time Heather said it.

Guilt stabbed at her. Heather needed her, and she was running away like a coward. She should stay. Try to help her. It was the right thing to do.

"Okay." Heather shrugged, already turning away. "I'll see you in school tomorrow, then."

Becca escaped out the door. The echoes followed. *Dissident. Dissident. Dissident.*

She had a plan. She would drop the car off at home, and then she would go to the playground. Let her mind go blank for a while. Forget about her mom. Forget about what Heather had said.

But when she walked in the door, intending to toss the car keys inside and leave again, her mom was standing on the other side. Waiting for her.

"The two of us are going to spend some time together," said her mom, daring Becca to contradict her. "And we're going to fix this."

chapter ten

Becca sat on the park bench with her mom, watching the sun go down. This park was nothing like her playground. The trees were spaced at precise intervals, the grass got mowed every Saturday, and the playground equipment in the distance gleamed as the last rays of the sun glittered off the rust-free metal. Becca hadn't been here in years, not since the old brown grass had been replanted and the new swings and jungle gym had replaced a couple of splintery picnic tables.

The quiet beauty should have relaxed her. But she couldn't relax, not with her mom sitting next to her, deliberately looking away as she waited for Becca to make the first move.

Becca stared up at the red-tinged clouds, hardly seeing them. "Just say whatever you brought me here to say."

"I didn't bring you here to have the same old arguments

again," her mom replied, still looking at the sky. "I miss you. I don't like what's happening to us. I brought you here because if we don't work to get things back to the way they used to be, we'll never get there."

Becca brought her gaze back to earth, to her mom's earnest face. "You want me to just ignore all of it? The things you did, the things—" *The things I've learned?*

"I executed a couple of dissidents, Becca. That's all." Her soft tone took the hostility out of her words. She stood up. "But we didn't come here to argue about that again." She held out a hand to Becca. "Let's walk together."

Becca stood up to join her mom, but didn't take the hand she offered.

Her mom started walking down the path. "Do you remember when we used to come here and feed the ducks?"

Her mom's words immediately called the memory to mind. Becca cringed at the thought of that younger Becca with her hand clasped in her mom's much larger one, giggling as she threw bread to the ducks. She hadn't known then what her mom was capable of.

Now every time Becca looked at her mom she thought of Jake's mother. Of all the false confessions. Of Heather's parents, who had been dissidents but might also have been right.

If they had been dissidents, and Becca thought they had been right, what did that make Becca?

"What's the point of remembering that? They filled in the duck pond two years ago." She didn't want to think about the times she had been happy with her mom. She didn't want to remember how close they used to be. It would only remind her of what was missing. Heather, her mom... she was losing everyone.

Before all this, she would have gone to her mom for advice about Heather. Her mom would have known what to do.

Her mom sighed. "Are you going to keep pushing me away like this?"

As if what had happened were Becca's fault. As if Becca were the one who had killed people's parents, who had abandoned the truth in favor of whatever lies her bosses told her to feed to the dissidents.

"Don't you miss it at all?" her mom asked. "The time we used to spend together? The talks we used to have?"

Of course she did. But what was she supposed to do, make herself forget everything she had found out?

They walked together in silence for a couple of minutes as the sky grew darker.

Her mom's phone buzzed. Her mom picked it up and frowned at the display. "It's work."

"Do they want you to go in?" If her mom had to rush off to work, they could put this off until another time. Becca could arrange to be busy whenever that was.

"They can live without me for one night." She reattached the phone to her belt.

Becca couldn't remember ever seeing her mom ignore a call from work before.

"Things used to be a lot simpler, didn't they?" her mom mused. "Before work got so busy. Before this thing with Heather and Jake."

In school earlier, Becca had greeted Jake like she always did, and they had kept their conversation to safe topics like always. She hadn't mentioned what her mom had said about him and his family. She had told herself it was because they were in school, where anyone could overhear, but she knew better.

If he found out her mom had been the one to kill his mother, he wouldn't want anything to do with her. The memory of Heather's reaction was still fresh in her mind. But it wasn't just that. She didn't want to ask him if her mom's story was true because she didn't want to try to decipher his answers to figure out whether he was lying. She'd done enough of that lately. More than enough.

For one irrational second, she thought about asking her mom for advice.

Then she remembered again.

"It's not just you," her mom continued, as though Becca had answered her. "I miss the way things were before work got so crazy. Back when I could actually spend time with you."

"I miss it too," Becca admitted, even though she wasn't sure she wanted to respond. "It was nice when the most important thing in the world was feeding the ducks." But she didn't have go to back that far to find a time when things had been easier. She only had to go back a month, to before Heather's phone call.

In front of her, Becca saw the bench where they had sat and watched the sunset. The path had taken them in almost a complete circle.

"Things are harder for both of us now. Especially for you." Her mom slowed down. "But I want you to know I'm still here if you need me. If there's anything you want to talk about, anything you want to ask me, you can. About Jake's family, or what happened with Heather, or anything else."

Becca wished she could. But it wasn't as simple as her mom made it sound. Asking about what she had found on her mom's computer didn't just mean admitting she had gone snooping through her files. It meant admitting she knew something she wasn't supposed to know. Something Internal had kept secret for... how long? How long had they been doing this?

She was about to answer with some kind of noncommittal refusal when she stopped. Something was bothering her about what her mom had said, something besides how she wished she could take her mom up on her offer.

No, it wasn't about what her mom had said. It was about the way she had said it.

It reminded her of something. It reminded her of...

That conversation with Jake. The one where he'd asked her about Heather just a little too intently.

She had been wrong about Jake.

This time, she didn't think she was wrong.

"You're trying to find out if I'm a dissident."

Her mom said nothing.

Becca faced her. "That's why you brought me here. It had nothing to do with fixing things between us. You just wanted to get me to... what, ask you if the dissidents have been right all along?"

"I do want to fix things between us. And I want to make sure you're all right. I can see you changing, and it worries me." Her mom didn't change her tone, didn't break her calm. Of course she didn't. She did this with dissidents all the time.

Becca broke away from the path and took off running toward home.

* * *

Her mom caught up with her before she even made it out of the park.

She couldn't outrun her mom. There was no point in trying. She slowed down to let her mom walk beside her.

"I'm not a dissident."

Her mom could tell when she was lying. Did she see it now?

"I'm sorry I brought it up the way I did," said her mom. "I should have just asked. But considering the way things have been between us, I didn't know if you'd talk to me at all, let alone tell me the truth."

They left the park. As they moved onto the road, they started walking single-file: Becca in front, her mom behind.

"So this was all an act. Just a way to get me to let my guard down." With her mom behind her, out of sight, Becca almost felt like she was talking to herself.

"Not at all. Everything I said was true. I miss you, Becca."

And Becca missed her. Even knowing why her mom had really come out to the park with her didn't change that.

But the person she missed had never existed.

A car passed them, temporarily blinding Becca with its headlights. "I know something is going on," her mom said over the noise. "I know Heather and Jake have been telling you things." She lowered her voice as the car disappeared into the distance. "You're starting to wonder if they're right. It's understandable."

Heather and Jake. Her mom was going to try to blame this on them. Becca remembered what had happened the last time her mom had thought one of her friends was a dissident. She still had nightmares sometimes where Anna accused her of turning her over to Internal.

"They haven't——" Becca started.

Her mom spoke over her. "But some part of you knows that what they've been telling you is wrong. That's why it all seems so confusing. Whatever they've told you, I can explain it all for you if you just ask. If you don't talk to me, I can't help." Her voice, floating up from someplace behind Becca, was tight with restrained fear.

"Heather joined the Monitors. She wouldn't have done that if she was a dissident." But Becca had no way to defend Jake. Nothing to say that would save him if her mom decided the only way to keep him from passing dissident ideas to Becca was to have Internal arrest him again.

"I don't know who let that girl into the Monitors, but whoever did it is either an idiot or needs to be investigated. Not only were both her parents dissidents, now she's started spreading dissident ideology herself."

"All she's told me is that Internal was right to execute her parents!" She knew it was hopeless even as she said the words. Her mom wasn't going to drop this. She could see what was happening to Becca, and in her mind, the only reasonable explanation was that Heather and Jake were responsible. Nothing Becca said would change that.

Nothing she said about Heather and Jake, at least.

But if she admitted to finding the evidence...

Her mom would know she had been snooping. She would know that Becca had information she wasn't supposed to have.

But she would also know that Becca had gotten the information from her computer. Not from Heather or Jake.

"After what Anna told me..." Saying Anna's name felt like betraying her all over again. "I went on your computer one night when you were at work. I looked through your files.

And... I found something."

They were almost home. The glow of the parking lot illuminated the road ahead of them.

"One of the dissidents' files had information about what he was supposed to confess to. What you were supposed to make him say." Becca didn't know if her mom could hear her. She was speaking so softly she could barely hear herself.

Her mom's answer, when it came, was just as quiet. "We need to have a talk."

* * *

Neither of them said anything else as they walked through the parking lot and into the building. The stairwell was silent, but Becca couldn't think over the sound of her uneven breaths.

Becca followed her mom into the apartment. She felt like she was walking to her execution.

Her mom sat down on the couch. Becca joined her.

Was this how her mom looked when she was interrogating a dissident? That carefully-blank expression, those unreadable eyes?

Her mom spoke first. "I'm sorry for lying to you."

That wasn't how she had expected her interrogation to begin.

"I didn't want to do it," her mom continued. "But you have to understand, nobody outside Internal is supposed to know about this. It's not even well-known inside Processing. If anyone found out that you had this information... or that you got it from me..." A hint of fear crept into her too-neutral tone.

Becca kept quiet. She didn't need her mom finding out

about the conversation she'd already had with Heather.

"Dissidents have been passing around distorted versions of the truth for years," said her mom. "These things always make it back to them sooner or later. But it's important that everyone else believes it's just another dissident lie, if they hear about it at all; otherwise what we're doing would be meaningless. If that weren't so important, I would have told you the truth a long time ago. I never wanted to keep anything from you."

"It's not about you lying to me." Everything her mom had done, and she thought lying to Becca was the worst part? "It's about what you've been doing. All the false confessions." She had to force every word out of her mouth. Talking about this with Heather had been hard enough. To talk about it with her mom, with someone who worked for Internal, was practically unthinkable. But at the same time, something in her unclenched a little with every word she spoke. It felt good to talk to her mom again. To be able to tell her the truth.

She kept going. "I know you. You wouldn't do something like this. The truth matters too much to you." She met her mom's eyes, but only for a second. It was too hard to look at her. "But you've been doing it all along, haven't you?"

Her mom's phone buzzed again. Her mom ignored it.

"You need to remember something." Her mom got off the couch and knelt between Becca and the coffee table, so Becca had no choice but to look at her. "No matter whether these people have done what they've confessed to or not, they're still dissidents. We can simply execute them, or we can go a step further and use them to strengthen society. We choose the latter."

Becca had told herself the same thing, when she had first

found out. Those people were dissidents. They deserved whatever happened to them.

Dissident.

She went cold.

No. She wasn't like the people her mom was talking about. She hadn't done anything that would get her arrested. Right?

But what had Anna done?

Even if Becca had been telling the truth about her, Anna would only have been guilty of passing along a rumor she might not have even believed. Hadn't Becca given that same piece of information to Heather? Hadn't she done something more serious than that when she had gone through her mom's files?

"What about…" Her mouth was dry. "What about people who haven't done anything but say the wrong thing? People like Anna?" *People like me?*

"In instances like that, it makes even more sense for us to try to get something useful from them," her mom answered. "Those dissidents usually can't even give us the names of any others. Either way, we have to remove them from society. By using them this way, we can do some good as well as eliminating the harm they cause."

That was what she was now. That was what these thoughts made her. A dissident, no different from any other dissident in Processing. Somebody to get rid of. Somebody to use.

I'm not a dissident.

If she hated what her mom was doing, she was a dissident.

If she was a dissident, she was one of the people her mom was talking about.

"But how are you strengthening society by getting people to confess to things they haven't done?" *Please make it make sense,* she pleaded silently. *Please make me believe you.*

Stop me from turning into a dissident.

Her mom moved back up to the couch. "The first question you asked was about people who haven't done anything you would consider serious," she said. "That's exactly why what we're doing is necessary." She leaned toward Becca. "Most people think the way you do. If you heard someone say the country was better off under the old regime, what would you do?"

"I'd report them," she said immediately. But was that even true anymore?

Just how far gone was she?

"Why?" asked her mom.

"Because only a dissident would think something like that." She didn't see how closely her words echoed Heather's until she heard herself speak.

"But what makes that dissident dangerous?" her mom pressed.

Becca hesitated, not sure how to answer.

"Right," said her mom. "You wouldn't be able to say. One person, making an offhand comment about the government, doesn't look like a threat. A conspiracy to overthrow the government—that's the kind of threat people understand."

"The kind of threat you create."

Her mom nodded. "And because people believe that those conspiracies exist, they understand the danger that dissidents present, even if they understand it for the wrong reasons. It becomes automatic. When they hear someone saying the country was better off with the former government, they know that person is a danger to society, even if they don't consciously think about why."

"But what makes those people dangerous to begin with?" If she could find what made even the minor dissidents dangerous, maybe she could find the thing that separated her from them.

"A thousand tiny drops of poison will kill somebody as easily as a giant spoonful," her mom answered. "But those tiny drops are harder to see. If people become complacent toward dissidents who don't appear to pose any immediate threat, soon they'll start ignoring them. If the dissidents are ignored instead of stopped, they'll have a chance to gain enough power that people will stop ignoring them and start listening. And the more people listen to them, the more powerful they'll become. Before you know it, with no conspiracy necessary, we'll have exactly what we had before. Chaos, corruption, a world built on ignorance and fear."

Becca wanted to believe her. She wanted to believe that what Internal was doing—what her mom was doing—was right, no matter how many lies were involved, no matter what her mom had to do to get dissidents to say what she needed them to say. If she could just make herself believe it, she could have her mom back. She could have her mind back. She could have her life back.

Heather had done it. She had blocked out all her grief, blocked out everything Becca had told her. She had convinced herself that her parents had deserved to die. Why couldn't Becca convince herself that her mom was doing the right thing?

Her mom's neutral mask slipped a little more, revealing the fear underneath, with every second she waited for Becca's response.

"I think I get it," said Becca slowly. "You have to do what

you're doing, so people will understand that dissidents are dangerous. Otherwise they won't see the danger until it's too late."

Her mom sagged against the back of the couch, letting all her muscles relax at once. "Exactly."

"I think I need some time to think about this," said Becca. "It's a lot to absorb." She swallowed. "Thanks for explaining. I should have asked you when I first found out."

She escaped to her room before her mom could look past her relief to wonder whether Becca meant what she had said.

* * *

Sometime around midnight, Becca's mom answered the call from work after all. From behind her bedroom door, Becca assured her that it was fine for her to leave, that she didn't need to talk anymore. After the apartment door closed behind her mom, she waited five minutes before she left the apartment herself.

She hadn't ever gone to the playground this late before. Stepping away from the lighted parking lot and onto the dark road, she was reminded of the time she had walked to 117 to find Heather. The night that had started all this.

That night, she'd had a purpose. Find Heather. Help her. Tonight she didn't know what she was looking for. She used to be able to escape her problems at the playground, but this time she carried the problem with her. Where could she go to escape her own mind?

Dissidents were dangerous. Becca knew that. She had known it all her life.

Becca thought like them. She talked like them. She acted

like them. Was she dangerous?

Becca sped up, trying to outrun her thoughts.

Dissidents would destroy the government if Internal didn't stop them. They would replace justice and order with chaos and corruption.

What did that even mean?

Did a world built on justice and order, the world her mom had taught her to believe in, involve people like Anna being arrested? People like Jake's mom being tortured to death? People who said one wrong thing forced to confess to trying to overthrow the government?

She felt like she had run straight off a cliff. Her feet hit the solid pavement with every stride, but she could still feel herself falling.

She couldn't start thinking like this. She had to stop this somehow.

She slowed as she reached the playground. At night, it looked downright sinister. Elongated shadows stretched out from the swing set poles and reached for her along the ground. The playhouse had transformed into a black hole ready to suck her in.

A shrill warble, too close to be a bird, cut through the silence.

Her heart nearly exploded out of her chest.

The noise came again, but this time she recognized it. Her phone. Right. Glad nobody was around to witness her moment of panic, she answered. "Hello?"

"Hey." It was Jake, sounding more subdued than she had heard him since the day he'd told her about his past. "I know it's late, but... I need to talk to you. Or just hang out. Or something." His voice wavered. "Do you think you could meet me at the old playground by your building?"

She stopped walking. Jake never sounded like this when he called her. Ever since he had explained his history to her, they had kept their conversations almost obsessively casual. He never called her sounding upset, or asked her to come hang out this late at night. Something had to be wrong.

But with her mom's explanation circling through her head, with her desperate denials no longer working, she had no room for talking to Jake, for forcing what her mom had said about him out of her mind.

Fighting her guilt, she opened her mouth to tell him she couldn't make it.

A figure stepped out of the playhouse. He waved as he walked toward her.

Jake was already here. And now he knew she was here too.

At first he was only a vague shadow. As she got closer, his features resolved. His familiar face, minus his usual smile. The tears that glittered in his eyes.

The ring of bruises around his neck.

Becca started to reach her hand up toward them, then let it fall back to her side. "What happened?"

Jake shifted awkwardly on his feet. "It was a bad day. That's all."

She tried to keep her mind on Jake's problems, tried to block out the questions that still wouldn't leave her alone. "Bad days don't usually involve someone trying to strangle you."

Jake walked the few steps to the swings and sat down. The swing creaked under his weight. "It's just my dad. Sometimes he's almost normal, and sometimes he's... not. Today when I got home from school, he thought I was from Internal." He clutched the rusted chains and let the swing sway back and forth. "I managed to remind him who I was, but after that it was like I wasn't there. He kept talking to my mom and Sarra, like they were there in the room with him. I stayed as long as I could, but I had to get out of there. And you were the only person I could go to." He laughed. Something about his laugh didn't sound quite sane.

Becca knew she should try to comfort him. but all she could think about was the name he had said. "Sarra. Your sister?"

He nodded.

His sister. She had existed after all. Which meant her mom had been right, at least about that part of his story. And if she had been right about that part, why not about all of it?

It didn't matter what he had or hadn't told her. Not right now. He needed her.

But if she ignored this, it would mean she didn't care that he might have been a dissident. That he might still be a dissident. And that would mean she was turning into somebody who could forgive dissident activity but not a few false confessions, somebody who hung around dissidents as if she were one of them.

Again she felt herself falling.

It was already too late.

No. She could stop this.

She took a step back. "You never told me about her."

"I'm sorry." He scuffed his foot along the ground. "I meant to."

"You told me you weren't actually dissidents."

Now he looked up at her, his eyes wide, the moonlight lending them an eerie glow. "We weren't. I explained what happened."

"Mom told me there was nobody staying with you. She said your sister was involved with a dissident group. She said all of you were dissidents."

Tell me she was wrong, she begged inside her mind, just like she had earlier during her mom's explanation. *Make me believe you.*

It didn't work any better now than it had then.

Jake didn't speak. His swing stopped moving.

It was true. She knew it just looking at him, just listening to the silence between them.

"I didn't know what else to do." His words faded into the air. "You were going to leave unless I explained, but if I told you the truth…"

She wanted to forgive him. She wanted to tell him that it was all right, and that she understood, and that she was sorry for everything that had happened to him today and in all the time since his arrest.

But how, after hating her mom for lying about something Internal had ordered her to keep secret, could she forgive Jake for lying about *this?*

How could she justify that?

"I told you not to lie to me." The coldness in her voice made her shudder. She sounded like her mom.

Better to sound like her mom than like a dissident. Right?

"What was I supposed to tell you?" His voice roughened. "Was I supposed to say they shot my sister on TV as some kind of lesson? Was I supposed to tell you how it was her fault all along for getting involved with those useless people who were willing to just throw us away afterwards?" He was yelling now. "Was I supposed to tell you how little it all meant to them, in the end? Everything we did for them, to expose this government for what it really is? Everything we went through? Was I supposed to tell you how they came to me after, and asked me to join them, when they weren't willing to help us in the only way that mattered?"

His words hung in the air, coloring the silence that grew between them as they both realized what he had said.

No lies this time. Nothing getting in the way of the truth.

Jake was a dissident.

What would you do if someone admitted to having contact with a dissident group? She wasn't sure if the voice in her mind was her mom's or her own.

I'd report him, of course.

Jake and his family hadn't been arrested by accident. They hadn't just said the wrong things in front of the wrong people, either. They had actively worked against the government. And even after Internal had let him go, Jake had been in contact with dissidents, and hadn't reported them. That alone meant he wasn't as harmless as Internal thought, wasn't harmless enough to be released. Becca tried to make herself see that, to make herself understand that he and his family had deserved everything that had happened. That turning him in, now that she knew he'd had contact with the group just like his sister, was the only right thing to do.

She couldn't.

He stood, trembling. "You're going to turn me in now." He said it flatly, like it was an undisputed fact.

"No," she said, and felt herself hit bottom. "I won't."

"I can't let that happen." He took a step toward her. "I told my dad I would protect him."

"I won't turn you in," she repeated, backing away. The

sound of her heartbeat filled her ears.

He kept advancing on her. "Why should I believe you?"

She had thought it would be difficult to say the words. Instead they fell from her mouth easily, almost eagerly. "Because I'm a dissident too."

He crossed the final distance to her.

And wrapped his arms around her as she collapsed in silent tears.

chapter eleven

"You may think dissidents don't care about schools," said Mr. Adams as he shut the classroom door. "After all, why would a bunch of kids matter to them? But if you think that, you're wrong."

The Citizenship classroom smelled like chalk and sweat. The breeze coming through the window wasn't enough to dispel the stale air. Around Becca, her classmates fidgeted at their desks—except for Heather, who was already scribbling down notes.

Failing to report dissidents is a crime, warned the poster that hung beside the blackboard. Becca squirmed until she remembered no one could see how she had changed.

"I don't know how many of you remember what happened eight years ago," Mr. Adams continued. "Internal discovered that across the country, dissidents had infiltrated the school system by becoming teachers and were using their influence to pass their ideology on to their students."

Becca did remember that. Her third-grade teacher had disappeared, and for the rest of the year they'd had a series of incompetent substitutes, from the one who kept forgetting the times tables to the one who burst into tears when someone threw a wadded-up piece of paper at her. Now, of course, Becca knew the truth. Internal had almost certainly manufactured the supposed dissident conspiracy. Had Becca's teacher even been a dissident, or had Internal started arresting innocent people?

She turned the thought around in her mind for a moment, waiting for the accusing voice. It didn't come.

Dissident. The word didn't scare her anymore.

"Yesterday, Internal learned that the same thing has started happening again. In more than a hundred schools—including many elementary schools—dissidents have been teaching anti-government sentiments to their students, and in some cases even recruiting students into dissident groups."

How many people had Internal framed to make this conspiracy look real? How many false confessions had they gotten? Anger boiled up in her again, but this time, it felt good. It felt honest. She wasn't using it to block out the truth anymore.

She mouthed the word, testing it out. *Dissident.*

A smile threatened at the corners of her lips. She forced her face to stay neutral, knowing how it would look if she smiled at the mention of a dissident conspiracy.

"These dissidents saw schools as places full of young impressionable minds. They looked at people like you and saw potential recruits, naïve kids whose minds they could poison with their lies."

No, that was how Internal saw them. That was why they had classes like this in the first place—to get them to believe whatever Internal wanted them to believe. Becca twitched her legs, suddenly restless. Now that she understood, how could she keep sitting here as though nothing had changed?

"But they underestimated you." The teacher struck the chalk against the blackboard for emphasis, leaving a single white dot. "Do you know who brought this conspiracy to Internal's attention? It was the students in the schools that had been infiltrated."

There hadn't even been a conspiracy. It was all a lie.

Next to Becca, some boy she didn't know spun his pencil on his desk. Over by the window, Laine passed a note to another girl, who covered her mouth to hide her giggles. Somebody scraped his chair back and forth along the floor. The clock above the door ticked out the seconds until the final bell.

Just like yesterday, and the day before, and the day before that.

Mr. Adams stopped in the middle of his speech about watching other teachers for signs of dissident sympathies. "Becca? Are you paying attention?"

Becca brought her gaze back to the front of the room. "Yeah. Sorry."

"What's the first thing you should do if you suspect a teacher of having dissident sympathies?"

Hope that they do. Hope that they really can convince everybody here of the truth. "Report them."

"What if you're not sure whether a teacher is a dissident or not?"

"Report them. Internal will be able to figure it out better than I can." The same answer she would have given yesterday. And the day before. And the day before that.

Mr. Adams, satisfied, nodded and returned to his lecture.

The clock ticked away another few seconds.

She was a dissident... and it didn't mean a thing.

* * *

For the rest of the week, Becca sat in class like always, and stayed quiet like always. She and Jake ate together at lunch and talked about nothing, their secret hovering unspoken in the background. She sat at home alone over the weekend, hoping her mom wouldn't get back from 117 before she went to bed, then fighting nausea as she remembered just what her mom was doing at work all day. She paced back and forth in her room; it did nothing to dispel her growing restlessness. At school on Monday, her teachers kept telling her to pay attention.

Monday night after dinner, she watched executions, listened to the dissidents recite their meaningless confessions. Tuesday and Wednesday she left the TV off. She could still hear them.

On Thursday, two teachers disappeared.

They probably hadn't even been dissidents. Or if they were, they hadn't been part of this giant conspiracy like everyone was saying.

What did it matter? Knowing the truth hadn't let Becca save them.

"Thanks for inviting me over," said Heather as she walked into Becca's room. "I've missed you. It feels like I haven't been here in ages."

No hint that she remembered their argument. It was as if it had never happened. Becca paced from the door to the bed and back again. "I need to talk to you."

Heather fingered her Monitor pin. "Is it about what happened at school? The teachers who were arrested?"

For the first time in a week, Becca felt something approximating hope. Maybe she was going to be able to do this after all. Maybe it would even be easier than she had thought. She couldn't save those teachers, or anyone else in 117, or the dissidents on TV, but maybe she could save Heather.

"I was hoping you'd come to me," said Heather.

"You were?" Maybe her attempts to get Heather to acknowledge what they had found hadn't been futile after all. Maybe Heather had finally realized what a mistake this Monitor thing was.

Heather nodded. "And I think you should do it."

Becca blinked.

"It's worth it," Heather assured her. "I finally feel like I'm doing something useful. Something important. And with everything that's going on, we need all the help we can get."

It took a couple of seconds for Heather's meaning to sink in. "You want me to join the Monitors."

Heather looked perplexed. "Isn't that what you wanted to talk to me about?"

"No." Becca started pacing again. Touch the door, pass

Heather, touch the bed. Pass Heather again. She forced herself to stop, to restrain her restless energy. "I wanted to talk to you about your parents."

Heather's face darkened. "They're gone. They got what they deserved. What is there to talk about?"

"I remember what you said last time we talked." Becca drummed her fingers on her desk. "You told me you're only doing all this because otherwise you wouldn't be able to deal with what happened to them. But you're helping the people who killed them. It doesn't make any sense."

Heather frowned. "What are you talking about? I never said anything like that."

Denying everything just like Becca's dad. What stories did Heather tell herself to help her forget why she had really joined the Monitors? Did she try to make herself believe she had always hated her parents? Did she tell herself that what happened to them was for the best because it made her understand what was really important?

Becca kept going. She couldn't give up now. "Do you really think this is what they would want?" Her voice grew louder and higher until the last word turned into a hysterical shout. She clamped her lips shut. She didn't want to yell at Heather. She just had to do something. It was hard enough to watch the executions go on exactly like they had before she knew the truth, to see people disappear and know that her new understanding did nothing to help them. She couldn't keep watching Heather slip away too.

"Why does it matter what they would want?" While Becca struggled to keep from pacing, Heather held herself like a statue. Every muscle was tensed, as if she thought she might have to bolt at any second.

Becca was fighting a battle she couldn't win. The old Heather was gone. It was too late to save her from what she had become.

But it was the only battle she could fight.

She took a deep breath. Calmed her voice. "Wouldn't it make more sense to try and do something to fight the people who killed them, instead of turning into one of them?"

Like what? There was nothing Heather could do. Nothing Becca could do.

"Becca... you're scaring me." Heather started to take a step toward her, then stopped. "That dissident stuff you were saying last week was bad enough. I figured I must have misunderstood or something. I mean, I know you. You're not a dissident. But now... what are you saying? Fighting Internal? Fighting the government? What's happening to you?"

Becca saw her own helpless frustration reflected in Heather's eyes.

"Please tell me you're not saying what it sounds like you're saying." Heather looked down at her Monitor pin. "I don't want to have to turn you in."

If Becca dropped this, if she let Heather slip away, she would be giving up not just her best friend, but her only chance of saving somebody from Internal.

If she kept going, Heather might turn her in.

No. Heather wouldn't turn her in. Heather was her best friend.

Heather was a Monitor now.

"I didn't mean it." Becca looked down at the floor. "I don't even know what I was saying."

She could almost feel a disturbance in the air as her last chance to save Heather, her last chance to save anyone, slipped away.

* * *

Becca stared at the TV, only half-seeing it. She didn't even know what she was watching. She should go to bed, she knew; it was probably after midnight by now. But last night she'd had another nightmare about Anna, and she could still feel the dream lurking in her subconscious, ready to torment her again tonight. If she managed to sleep. She knew the restlessness would return as soon as she got into bed, and she'd toss and turn and end up pacing her room at three in the morning.

The apartment door opened.

Becca should have gone to bed when she'd had the chance. That would have made eight straight days of not having to look at or talk to her mom.

"I'm glad to see you," her mom mumbled as she sank down onto the couch. "It's been, what, a week?"

"Something like that." Becca tried to focus on the TV. An Enforcer raced down a city street in pursuit of... Becca didn't know. Something important.

"It's good to see a friendly face. It feels like it's been a hundred years since I've seen someone who doesn't want to kill me."

Becca kept her face blank. She didn't think she could manage friendly. "I was just going to bed."

"If it's because of me, you don't need to worry about it. I don't care how late you stay up. If it were a problem, your grades wouldn't be so high." She sank deeper into the couch. "Sleep does sound tempting, though."

"Maybe we should both go to bed." Now the Enforcer was handing a struggling dissident over to a woman who looked kind of like Heather. Becca flicked off the TV.

Her mom let out a groan and closed her eyes. "You wouldn't believe what this week has been like. I swear every impossible dissident was arrested on the same day, and they all got assigned to me."

"It's late," Becca said, standing up. "And I have a test tomorrow."

Her mom used to rant about work to her all the time. How had she never thought before about what it meant? How had she never imagined who the dissidents her mom complained about were, and what her mom was doing to them?

Back then, they had just been dissidents. That was the difference. Only dissidents; barely even human.

Back then, Becca hadn't been one of them.

"Just when I was finally getting somewhere with one of them—which took the better part of four days while I fell behind on everything else—Public Relations swooped in and snatched him up for execution." She let out her breath in frustration. "He had connections we've been waiting a year to find, but did that matter to them? No, all that mattered was that they needed someone young to balance out the age range in their latest batch of executions."

Becca wondered how suspicious it would look if she ran to her room and locked the door.

"I would gladly have given them the man who came in with him. That one would say he was innocent if he had been arrested with dissident pamphlets in one hand and a bomb in the other. But no, he's too old, and now the directors want me to get enough useful information out of him to make up for losing the other one."

What if she threw the remote at the TV and smashed it? How suspicious would that look?

"Then there's the whole teacher thing." She massaged her temples as she spoke. "One good thing about you going through my files—at least I can talk to you about these things now."

What if she threw the remote at her mom's head?

"Every teacher who says something suspicious in class—and the sheer number of dissident teachers we've found is enough to make me want to pull you out of school—now has to be used for this project. It wouldn't be so bad if it were something local, but we have to coordinate with processing centers across the country. We got a great confession from one of the teachers—all he needed was a little prompting and he came up with the entire thing himself—but it contradicted something Processing 103 had used, so we couldn't use any of it."

Becca's breathing grew louder in her ears. Her hands twitched with the effort of keeping them still. She had to move. She had to do something.

"And Public Relations keeps changing what they want. First they wanted to emphasize the heroism of the students who reported the dissident teachers. Then they decided it would be better to place more emphasis on the students who had already been corrupted, and show the damage that had been done, so Enforcement focused their attention on high-school-age dissidents. Now Public Relations isn't sure whether they want to go in that direction after all, so we're left with these extra dissidents and nothing to use them for—but we can't execute them, in case the geniuses in Public Relations change their minds again."

"Stop it! I don't want to hear about this!" Becca hadn't meant to start yelling. She hadn't even meant to open her mouth.

Her mom, about to say something else, stopped with her mouth half-open.

"I don't want to know what you're doing in that place. I don't want to think about it." *Shut up,* she told herself. *Shut up, shut up, shut up.* But she kept going, as though her mouth had disconnected itself from her brain. "I want you to be who you used to be, not some... *torturer.*" The word fell heavily from her lips. Her dad had used it, in one of the last fights before he had moved out.

"Becca——" her mom started.

The image of Jake clutching the chains of the swing, bruises around his neck, flashed in front of her eyes. Her mom had done that to him, by doing much worse to the rest of his family. "I don't care what those people said!" she screamed, while the rational part of her brain looked on in horror. "I don't care what they did! If they're working against the government, let them! Maybe if they took over, people wouldn't disappear for no reason!"

In the silence, Becca's heartbeat echoed so loudly that she couldn't imagine how her mom didn't hear it.

Her mom stared at her with wide wounded eyes, betrayed eyes, as though Becca had stabbed her in the gut.

There would be no talking her way out of it this time. It was too late for that.

Maybe too late for anything.

How long now before she ended up in 117?

Between protecting Becca from Internal and protecting

society from another dissident, which would her mom choose?

She didn't know the answer.

"Becca." Her mom spoke her name in a strangled whisper.

Becca didn't wait to hear what she would say next.

She ran.

chapter twelve

A month and a half ago, Becca's phone had woken her in the middle of the night. She answered before she was fully awake. Heather didn't say anything at first. When she did speak, her voice was choked with sobs; she stopped every few words to take another strangled whimpering breath.

Becca could only understand a few words here and there. Disconnected fragments, half-intelligible. Nothing that made any sense. Nothing that told Becca what had happened. She offered what little comfort she could, and gripped the phone tighter every time Heather said something else she couldn't decipher.

"Please come," Heather managed through her hysteria. "Please."

Still murmuring reassurances, Becca left the apartment.

She padded down the hall and rang Heather's doorbell, not caring if she woke Heather's parents. Nobody answered.

"I'm right outside," said Becca. "Answer your door." Maybe it wasn't locked. Becca reached for the doorknob.

The door was hanging slightly open.

Through the phone, a series of louder sobs, interspersed with breaths so fast Becca thought Heather might pass out.

"Where are you? Just tell me where you are and I'll come find you."

No response except more gasping breaths.

Becca nudged the door open the rest of the way and stepped inside. An eerie quiet hung over the living room. She flicked on the lights.

The couch had been gutted. White stuffing spilled out from the cushions onto the floor. Books, pulled from the bookshelf seemingly at random, littered the floor. The computer that normally sat in the corner was gone, wires spilling across the desk where it used to be.

She thought she heard Heather gasp, then realized the sound had come from her own throat.

This couldn't be what it looked like.

"Whatever is going on, I'll help you," said Becca. "I promise. Just tell me where you are."

A long pause. Then, finally, a clear sentence—one she had never imagined hearing.

"I'm at 117."

Now, six weeks and an eternity later, Becca sat in the corner of the playhouse, knees pulled up to her chest. She dialed Heather's number with trembling fingers.

Moonlight shone through the slim rectangle of the doorless entrance. A spider skittered across the illuminated part of the floor, away from Becca, across the pattern her shoes had made in the grime. Becca squeezed closer against the wall.

"Hello?" Heather's bleary mumble sounded like it was coming from outer space.

Becca tried to speak. Nothing came out. Finally, too late, her mouth had gotten the message to stop talking.

"Hello?" Heather repeated. "Becca?"

"It's me." Becca barely recognized her own voice.

"What's going on?" Heather asked through a yawn.

"I'm at the playground." She whispered the words without meaning to. As though if she spoke any louder, Internal would hear and come for her.

"What are you doing there this late?" Heather's voice was thick with sleep and confusion. "Are you okay?"

"I need—" She needed the old Heather. That was who she had tried to call. Instead she had gotten this stranger, the one who had talked about turning her in.

"What do you need? What happened?"

Why had she called Heather? She knew who Heather was now. What she was.

"Never mind," she said, still in a whisper. "It's nothing."

She hung up—and dialed the number she should have called in the first place.

* * *

Jake sat with her for hours. He listened to her explanation of what had happened with her mom, and all her fears about what might happen. When she had nothing else to say, he sat with her in silence.

Becca glanced at her watch. Three in the morning. Was her

mom out looking for her? Was she sitting in the living room, waiting for her to come back? Or was she already at work again, torturing a confession out of another innocent person?

"Is there anything I can do?" Jake asked, the first thing he'd said in… she didn't know how long.

Becca opened her mouth to say no. There was nothing he could do to make her mom forget what Becca had said to her. There was nothing he could do to make Becca less helpless; he couldn't give her the ability to save herself and all the other dissidents Internal tortured and killed.

But that wasn't entirely true, was it? He did have something he could do for her.

"I need you to give me something." She spoke quickly; she needed to get the words out before she could talk herself out of this.

"What do you need?"

"Contact information for the other dissidents you were involved with," she said in a rush.

Jake started shaking his head before Becca had finished speaking. "No. I'll give you anything else, but not that."

So close. She was so close to finding a way out of this intolerable in-between… but Jake could stand between her and the solution forever if he wanted to. "I have to do something. I can't keep going like this, knowing the truth and not being able to do a thing to change any of it. If my mom… if she really does report me… then it won't matter. But if she doesn't…"

"You don't want to get involved with them." Jake brushed away a fly that had landed on her leg. "They're useless. They had my sister set up that newspaper, but for what? What good did it ever do? And after what happened, they wanted me to help them like my sister had, but they wouldn't do anything to help us." The fly landed on his arm. He smacked it so hard his hand left a red mark where it had struck.

Part of her wanted to give up and leave it at that. But what would she do then? Keep going the way she had been? A week of this had made her boil over. How was she supposed to keep it up for the rest of her life?

"Anything is better than nothing," said Becca. "At least they're doing something."

"Something that could get them arrested. Do you understand the danger you'd be putting yourself in?"

"I'm already in danger just for the things I've already said. Heather could easily have reported me for what I said to her. My mom might still report me."

"You really don't get it, do you?" Jake shifted so he was sitting in front of her instead of beside her. "With your mom in Internal, you've been untouchable your whole life. You think you're still untouchable. You think actually fighting the government is the same as saying the wrong thing to somebody."

"Saying the wrong thing to somebody could get me arrested just as easily. It happens all the time. If I'm in danger anyway, I might as well do something that matters."

"You don't have a clue how things actually work outside the little bubble you've been living in. I bet you think everyone believes all the propaganda Internal puts out, don't you? Now you've finally figured out what Internal is really like, and you think you're going to save the world. Good luck with that—but don't expect me to help you get yourself killed."

Was Jake right about her? Was she too naïve to understand what this would mean?

She didn't care. She had to keep herself from ending up like her dad, forced to deny her dissident thoughts not only to protect herself but to stay sane.

"What do you think I should do, then? Just sit back and pretend none of it is happening? I have to do something!"

"This isn't some kind of game! Have you forgotten what happened to my sister? To my mother?" This was the Jake who had threatened Laine, the one who had thrown Becca out of his house.

But this time, Becca didn't shrink away.

"Of course not!" Her voice rose to match his. "Why do you think I want this? I can't just ignore what's happening and get on with my life as if nothing's changed. If that's all I'm going to do, why does it matter what I believe? I might as well do what Heather wants and join the Monitors."

"What do you think you'll really be able to do to make a difference?" Jake pried at a rusty nail sticking out of the floor.

Embarrassed to admit that she didn't have any idea, Becca crossed her arms. "More than I'm doing now."

"The answer is no. That's not going to change." He tugged harder; the nail popped free. He dropped it and started pulling loose splinters from the wood.

Becca could feel it again, the restless energy surging through her limbs, asking her why she wasn't doing anything with this new knowledge she had. She forced herself not to get up. "It's not your job to protect me." She fidgeted. "Please," she said, knowing how desperate she sounded. "Let me have this."

"What do you expect me to do?" Jake's voice hovered somewhere between challenge and defeat. "Hand over a resistance group to Raleigh Dalcourt's daughter?"

She jerked back as if he had slapped her.

She had called him here, confided in him, let him comfort her… and this was what he thought of her? That she was, what, faking all of it? That if he gave her what she had asked for, she would turn around and give it to her mom?

"You think I'm spying for Internal." The same thing she had thought about him at first. It was almost funny.

"No," said Jake. "I don't. I believe every word you've told me. But… I can't take the chance."

Becca wished she couldn't understand. She wished she couldn't see the distinction. It would make things easier. At least then she could channel some of her energy into raging at Jake.

But if she were in his position, she wouldn't want to take the chance either.

No matter what she said, no matter how much he trusted her, she was still her mother's daughter.

She wanted to scream.

She nodded. Her restrained energy made the motion jumpy and unnatural. "I understand."

She didn't want to admit it, but a tiny part of her was relieved.

The rest of her wanted to tear the playhouse apart.

She drummed her fingers against the floor. It didn't help. Her fingers came away coated in dust and unidentifiable grime. She wrinkled her nose and wiped her hands off on her jeans.

Jake looked at his watch. "I don't want to leave you, but I need to get home. I don't like leaving my dad alone for this long."

She let him go without protest. His presence wasn't

comforting anymore. Seeing him there, knowing he could give her a way out of this but wouldn't, only fed her frustration.

In the doorway, Jake stopped. "I'm sorry."

"I said I understand."

He didn't leave. "Be careful, okay? Maybe you shouldn't go home. Just in case."

"I'll figure it out." *Please just get out of here.*

With one last reluctant look, he left, and she was alone again.

Right back where she had started.

What now? She couldn't hide in this playhouse forever. But if she went home, there were two possibilities—either she'd go back to the way things were before, to unsuccessfully trying to keep herself from exploding, or she'd end up in an underground cell in 117. And she had no way of knowing which it would be.

The walls she had cowered against a couple of hours ago now felt like they were closing in on her. She stood convulsively and all but ran the couple of steps out the door.

And found herself staring at a wide-eyed, white-faced Heather.

* * *

"How long have you been here?" Becca asked. But the look on Heather's face told her everything she needed to know.

"Long enough." Heather was looking at her like she was a stranger. A monster.

A dissident.

"After your phone call, I couldn't sleep." She spoke quietly, but the stillness of the night air amplified her words. "I kept worrying about you. I knew you said it was nothing, but you sounded like something was seriously wrong. And after everything you did for me, I figured I owed it to you to at least find out if you were okay. So I took my aunt's car and drove down here." She stopped.

"And you heard me talking to Jake," Becca finished.

"I hid when he came out," said Heather. "After that, I wanted to come in and talk to you, but... I didn't know what to say."

Becca scrambled for some explanation she could give Heather, something to make her conversation with Jake seem innocuous. She came up with nothing.

Moonlight glinted off Heather's Monitor pin, giving the metallic eye a vicious gleam.

Maybe Becca didn't need to worry about her mom reporting her after all. Maybe Heather would do it before her mom had a chance.

And what about Jake?

This was Becca's fault. She had called Heather and then asked Jake to come here. She had asked Jake for the contact information. She was responsible for whatever Heather had overheard—and whatever happened to Jake because of it.

The question was on Becca's lips, but she couldn't ask it. *Are you going to turn us in?*

"Jake isn't even working with the dissidents," she said instead. "You heard him—he doesn't want to help them."

"But he hasn't reported them. That makes him as guilty as they are." She paused. "And if I don't turn you in, I'm as guilty as you are."

She was going to do it. She was going to report them.

The playground looked the same as it had on that night a week ago when she had finally admitted she was a dissident, but the shadows didn't unsettle her now. Patterns of light and darkness on the ground weren't threatening. The real threat was standing in front of her—her best friend, ready to make the phone call that would kill her.

"I kept wondering why you were saying all those things about Internal." The look on Heather's face reminded Becca of the way she had looked at her mom after she had found the evidence in that file. "I told myself you were still upset about what happened to my parents, and you weren't thinking clearly. Or that maybe your mom had told you to test me. I guess I didn't want to see the truth about you."

Becca fought the urge to run. What good would running do, anyway? "I just want to stop what happened to your parents from happening to anybody else. I know you keep telling yourself they deserved to die, but they didn't."

Heather rubbed her pin like it would protect her from Becca's words. "They were my parents. Not yours. You don't have any right to talk about what they did or didn't deserve."

Did Heather think Becca deserved to die, too? Becca didn't want to ask. She was afraid of the answer.

"I can't lose you like I lost them." Heather was almost talking to herself now. She stared at nothing. "I can't let you turn into what they turned into."

"If you report me, Internal will kill me," said Becca. "Just like them."

Heather didn't say anything.

All the years they'd spent together, and this was how it would end?

"After what happened to your parents, I did everything I

could to help you," Becca said into the silence. "Do this for me now. Don't turn us in." She heard herself as if from very far away. Heard the futility of her words.

Heather stood so still Becca wondered for a moment if she had simply shut down.

"I'm not going to turn you in," she said finally. She took both Becca's hands in her own. "I'm going to help you."

Becca almost melted with relief.

"Thank you," she said, but Heather was still talking.

"I thought this was about my parents. But it wasn't, was it? It was him. He did this to you."

"Jake?" No. This wasn't what was supposed to happen. Heather had said she wouldn't turn them in.

Or had she only meant she wouldn't turn *Becca* in?

"It has nothing to do with him." Becca's voice sped up as she tried to get the words out before it was too late, before Heather did something irrevocable. "I didn't even know about him until after. And he's not dangerous. He's not interested in fighting the government. All he wants to do is take care of his dad."

"He's a dissident." Heather spat the word. "But there might still be hope for you." She gripped Becca's hands tightly enough to cut off the blood flow. "You helped me. Now it's my turn to help you."

Becca pulled her hands away. "Please." But she had nothing to follow it up with, no way to convince Heather not to do this.

Becca had killed him.

"Do you understand what this will mean? What I'll be doing?" Heather touched the pin again, then jerked her hand away as if it had burned her. "Not turning you in, after what I heard… that's *dissident activity*, Becca. But I owe you too much not to give you this chance." She paused. "Please," she said, echoing Becca. "Don't waste it."

She rushed away, toward her aunt's car parked by the side of the road.

Becca had nothing to say, no magic words that would change Heather's mind. "Wait," she called after her. Useless. Meaningless.

Heather disappeared into the car and drove away.

chapter thirteen

Her mom's car wasn't in the parking lot.

Maybe she was out looking for Becca. Maybe she had gone to work. Either way, it didn't matter. What mattered was that Becca had to get to Jake's house as quickly as possible. With the car gone, that meant on foot.

She started running.

Calling him would look too suspicious. Surveillance would start monitoring his phone calls as soon as Heather reported him—if they weren't already listening in because of his history. Becca had to deliver her warning in person.

Out of the parking lot, onto the street. If anyone stopped her, what explanation could she give for going running in the middle of the night?

She turned onto the next street, already getting out of

breath. Already slowing down. She pushed herself harder, gasping, reminding herself why she had to get there in time. Thinking about Jake.

She had put him in danger. Now she was going to save him.

She would get there in time. She would save him. There was no other option.

The road was nearly empty at this time of night. She almost felt like she was the only person left in the world, until the occasional pair of headlights jerked her out of the illusion. The further she ran, the longer the road got, until it stretched to infinity, until she wondered whether she was covering any distance at all. Sometimes she looked down at her watch, expecting a minute or two to have gone by, and saw that she had lost five minutes, ten, twenty.

She slowed down, forced herself to go faster, slowed down again. She stopped, in tears, legs burning. Less than halfway there. She started running again; her leg wobbled underneath her, and she fell to the pavement. A car swerved around her. She crawled to her feet, her arm scratched and bleeding from her fall.

Heather must have reported him by now.

How long would it take for Internal to arrest him? Would they see him as a low priority and wait a few days, maybe a week or two, more than enough time for Becca to warn him? Or would he be like Anna—reported one night and gone the next morning?

Was it already too late?

She was going to save him.

There was no other option.

She dragged herself forward, feeling the road disappear behind her too slowly, watching the sky lighten ahead of her too quickly.

Halfway there.

Her legs burned, but she ignored the pain. It didn't matter. Only getting to Jake in time mattered.

Three-quarters of the way.

The sunrise streaked the sky with orange; Becca barely saw it. All she saw was one image, looping over and over in her mind: Enforcement at Jake's door, dragging him and his dad out of the house.

Almost there.

A car drove up behind her; it slowed as it got closer. Becca glanced over her shoulder.

Even in the dark, she recognized it. That was her mom's car.

So close. Another five minutes, maybe ten, and she would be there.

Her mom honked.

Becca pulled out her phone. She didn't care how suspicious it looked. If she didn't warn him now, she would never get the chance. She pretended she hadn't heard her mom as she dialed Jake's number.

His phone rang. And rang. Nobody there.

Too late.

No. There were plenty of reasons for him not to answer. He was probably asleep. Or with his dad. Or... or something. Something besides what she was afraid of.

"Hey." Jake's voice. Becca's heart leapt. She started to answer, but Jake kept talking. "It's Jake. Leave me a message and I'll get back to you when I can."

Just his voicemail.

Her mom leaned on the horn.

Becca tried to keep her voice light. Tried to sound like she wasn't afraid for Jake's life. "Hey, I know you said you weren't going to school today, so I thought you might want to hang out. You need to get out of the house. It'll be... boring there. Really boring." She could only hope that he would remember their date and the association of "boring" with "Internal," that he would hear the message underneath the words. *Go. Get out of there. Internal is coming.*

Her mom rolled down the window. "Becca!"

Becca hung up the phone. It would have to be enough.

She stayed where she was. Her mom pulled up beside her and stopped the car. "Get in."

Becca obeyed, still thinking about Jake, wondering whether he would understand her message. Or if it would even reach him in time.

She didn't remember to be afraid for herself until the car door's lock softly snapped into place.

* * *

They drove in silence.

Becca waited for her mom to say something. She didn't.

"Where are we going?" Becca finally asked.

Her mom didn't take her eyes off the road. "We're going to 117."

Becca felt her heart stop.

Her mom was giving her to Internal. Even as she had confided her worries about this very thing to Jake, she hadn't actually believed it could happen.

Was that what Jake had meant when he had accused her of seeing herself as untouchable?

"You're turning me in?" Her voice came out small and scared, a little girl's voice.

"No!" The car swerved. Her mom lowered her voice. "No. There's no need for that. You're not a dissident. You're just confused."

Relief fought with wariness. Could she trust what her mom told her? "Then why are you taking me to 117?"

"So I can help you." Her mom was gripping the steering wheel so tightly that her fingers had turned white.

Her mom... Heather... everyone wanted to help her. Heather wanted to do it by reporting Jake. Her mom wanted to do it by taking her to 117. Becca wished people would stop trying to help.

The road that had seemed so long a few minutes ago whizzed by outside. "What do you mean? Help me how?"

Her mom didn't say anything else.

The sunrise was starting to fade as they pulled into the parking lot of 117. Her mom got out of the car without a word. Becca followed only because she knew her mom would drag her if she didn't get out on her own.

They walked toward the building—not to the front door, the one Becca had used when she had come here to find Heather, but to a smaller door along the right-hand wall. Becca's legs shook from fear and exhaustion. Her heart sped up with every step she took that brought her closer to the building.

What had her mom meant about helping her?

Her mom took a card out of her wallet and slid it into the card reader by the side of the door. The door clicked open. Her mom stepped inside; again, Becca had no choice but to follow her.

They stepped into a small square room, with white walls to either side and an elevator in front. Her mom slid her card into the card reader beside the elevator. The elevator doors opened silently.

The elevator hummed as it descended. Becca's limbs twitched. She had to get out of here, before it was too late, before...

The elevator came to a stop.

The doors opened onto a gray hallway lit with dim yellow lights. The hallway stretched much further than the building above. Its rows of doors were broken up only by intersecting hallways.

The underground levels.

They stepped out of the elevator. Their footsteps echoed on the concrete floor. The hallway smelled like stale air and disinfectant.

The elevator doors closed behind them. No way out.

"What are we——" Becca's words echoed as loudly as her footsteps. She dropped her voice to a whisper. "What are we doing here?" She couldn't ask the rest of her question: *Why are we down here if you're not giving me to Internal?*

Had that been another lie?

"I need to show you something." Her mom didn't whisper like Becca, but somehow she kept her voice from traveling further than the two of them. "I need to show you what will happen to you if you keep going down the path you're on."

They walked through the maze of hallways, each one identical to the one before it, until Becca had no idea what direction the elevator was in, let alone how to get back there. Each hallway was deserted, silent except for their footsteps and the hum of the lights... and once, so faint Becca thought she must have imagined it, the sound of screaming from behind one of the doors.

They reached a dead end. At the end of the hallway, a man sat with his back against the wall, knees and elbows jutting out in all directions. His head hung down toward his chest; his eyes were closed. Becca thought he might be dead at first, until she heard a soft snore.

As they approached, he brought his head up with a start. "Raleigh! I didn't know you were here." He unfolded his limbs and clambered to his feet as quickly as his gangly legs would allow. Becca had to tilt her head up to see the blush spreading across his cheeks.

"I came in early," said her mom. "I was hoping you would still be here."

The man looked maybe ten years older than Becca, at most. His eyes traveled to Becca, to her arms hanging loosely at her sides. "Um, Raleigh? Are you sure that's safe?"

"She's not a prisoner," her mom answered sharply. "This is my daughter Becca."

"Oh! I'm sorry. I didn't mean..." His blush deepened. "It's nice to meet you," he said to Becca. "I'm Eli. I work with your mom." He turned his attention back to her mom. "Why were you looking for me? Did you need anything?" He asked the question as though her assigning him some task would be the highlight of his day.

Was this the moment of betrayal? Was her mom going to hand her over to this man and walk away?

"Are you still planning to execute prisoner K10-843 today?" her mom asked.

Jake. They've got Jake in here. That's why she brought me.

Eli nodded. "Why? Do you need her?"

Her. Not Jake after all, then. She let out a breath she didn't know she had been holding.

"No," her mom answered. "But I want you to let us watch."

Eli looked from her mom to Becca and back again, a question in his eyes.

"She's here for a school project," her mom lied smoothly. "With everything that's been going on in the schools, her Citizenship teacher thought an in-depth presentation on Processing would be appropriate, and Becca was the natural choice."

If Eli doubted her story, he didn't show it. "I can do it right now, if you want. I already brought her to room five."

Becca's mom nodded. "Lead the way."

So her mom had been telling the truth. She wasn't turning Becca over to Internal after all. She had brought Becca here to see a dissident executed, to show her what could happen to her.

Becca could handle that. She had seen executions on TV before. She was safe, and—for now, at least—so was Jake. That was what mattered.

Her stomach clenched.

She could handle this.

They traveled further into the maze, until they stopped at a door that looked the same as all the others. Becca's mom used her card to unlock the door. She walked in first, then Eli, who held the door open for Becca.

All she had to do was remind herself it was just like the executions on TV, and forget she was in the same room. Forget that her mom was right and she could easily end up dying just like this.

She could handle this. She could handle it.

She stepped inside.

The room wasn't much bigger than a closet. The same dim yellow light that shone in the hallways illuminated the gray concrete walls and the bloodstains someone had tried in vain to bleach off. Becca wanted to run, might have done it if Eli hadn't closed the door behind her.

The dissident lay crumpled in a corner, her hands cuffed behind her. Her tangled hair obscured her face. Burn marks traveled up her arm, disappearing under the sleeve of her grubby gray shirt. Her leg was twisted under her at an unnatural angle.

She raised her head; her hair fell away from her face. She looked up at them with unfocused eyes and

We haven't all decided you're a dissident. We just want to know what's going on.

blinked a couple of times before she

It's just one of those things she heard. You know how she is.

dropped her head back down to the floor.

Anna.

The air was too thick to pull into her lungs. Becca gasped for breath as Eli asked her mom, "Now?" As her mom nodded. As Eli took the gun from his belt and aimed it at Anna—

no no no, at the dissident in front of him, that's all this was, another execution—

aimed it at Anna and Becca covered her mouth to stifle her scream as Anna's head exploded against the wall.

chapter fourteen

Becca wasn't sure what happened after that. Only a few short flashes—retching as her mom led her through the hallways, then collapsing into the car with her ears still ringing, then her mom saying something she couldn't understand as they drove past the spot where she had tried to call Jake—interrupted the endless loop of Anna's death.

Her mom's phone rang as they reached their building. She argued with the person on the other end while Becca stayed perfectly still next to her and flinched at every angry word. After she hung up, she apologized for having to leave, promised they would talk about this later, asked Becca if she was sure she would be okay. Becca nodded and tried to give the right responses as Anna's death played over and over again in her mind.

She didn't remember getting out of the car. But suddenly she was standing in the parking lot, watching her mom drive away. Watching Anna get shot again and again.

There was something she needed to do. Something important.

Jake. Right. She had to look for Jake.

She started toward the playground. If Jake had gotten her message, if he had understood it... if it wasn't too late... that was where he would be.

She dragged herself down the road. She tried to run, but her legs wobbled underneath her, aching from her interrupted run to Jake's house, weak from the images still playing in her head. As she got closer to the playground, Jake's face replaced Anna's in her memory, until she could almost believe she had seen him die instead of Anna.

Anna. Becca had said one wrong thing, told one lie, and now Anna was dead. Because of her.

Was Jake in one of those rooms right now? Had Becca gotten him killed too?

When she reached the playground, she kept her head down at first, afraid of what she would see when she looked up—or rather, what she wouldn't see. She made herself raise her head. The weeds swayed in the breeze; the slide and swings sat deserted.

He could still be in the playhouse. Or he could have gone someplace else. Maybe he had thought the playground wasn't safe enough.

Or maybe Internal already had him.

She approached the playhouse, scrutinizing it for signs of life. Nothing. No noise, no movement. She stopped just outside the door, afraid to look inside, afraid to see it empty.

"Jake?" she called quietly.

She had expected silence; the answering voice made her jump. "Becca?"

He was here. Alive. Safe. Free.

Jake stepped out of the playhouse. He squinted as the light struck his face. "I heard footsteps. I thought you were Internal."

She kept her eyes fixed on his face as she walked up to him. She tried to let the reality of Jake in front of her—alive, safe, free—drive away the images in her head.

She didn't know if she kissed him first or if he was the one to reach for her. All she knew was that when his lips met hers, she could finally accept that he was real, that Internal hadn't taken him. Her visions of death—of Jake, of Anna, lying on the floor of that room as Eli raised his gun—faded into nothing as she pulled him closer. There was no Anna. No Internal. There was only her and Jake and the electric warmth spreading out from her lips through the rest of her body.

He stepped back, looking as dazed as Becca felt. "I need to check on my dad." He disappeared into the playhouse.

Becca followed him. Jake's dad was sitting in the corner where Becca had spent all of last night. His eyes were aimed in their direction, but whatever he saw, it wasn't them. His lips moved constantly, but no sound came out. Becca eyed him warily, remembering their last encounter. If he saw her, though, he didn't recognize her.

Jake followed Becca's gaze. "He's been like that since we left," he murmured. "I didn't tell him why we had to come here, but he knows."

"I was afraid you wouldn't understand my message."

"I got it." He watched his dad for a moment in silence.

Little by little, his muscles tightened. "Why are they after us? And how do you know about it?"

The last residual glow of the kiss disappeared as reality crashed back down over her. This was her fault. She had done this to them. Just like she had gotten Anna killed. "Heather overheard us talking last night."

She waited for Jake's condemnation. It didn't come.

He didn't say anything at all.

She tried to fill the silence. "I called her before I called you, and told her where I was. I know I shouldn't have done it. It was just... instinct. She was my best friend for so long." It hurt to say it in the past tense like that.

Still nothing from Jake. Becca couldn't even hear him breathing.

"She thinks you're turning me into a dissident. She thought she could save me by reporting you. I tried to talk her out of it, but it didn't work."

Still nothing.

"I'm sorry."

Nothing.

He squatted down next to his backpack, which lay on the floor beside his dad. He rummaged around until he pulled something out. Becca couldn't tell what he was doing. She wanted to offer more apologies, to say something, anything, that would get him to forgive her. She held herself back. She had already said all she could say.

A minute ago, their kiss had driven away her memories and her fears. Now they started crowding into her mind again, all pressing in on her at once. Too much.

She heard the sound of ripping paper and peered over Jake's shoulder. He was scribbling something down on a jagged-edged piece of notebook paper. A second later, he stood up.

"I was wrong not to trust you," he said. "You saved both our lives. If you hadn't warned me, Internal would have us both by now." A shudder ran through his body.

"It's my fault she overheard you in the first place," Becca protested.

"It doesn't matter. You saved us, even though you knew what would happen to you if Internal found out. Most people wouldn't have taken that risk." He pressed the strip of paper into her hand. "I should have given you this when you asked."

Becca looked down at the paper. All he had written on it was an unfamiliar phone number—but she knew what it was. The contact information she had asked him for.

She folded the paper and tucked it into her pocket. "Thank you."

It should have made her happy. But all she could think about was Anna.

The images pressed in closer.

She leaned in toward Jake, and the closer she got, the further away everything else felt. At the last second she hesitated, heart pounding, her lips inches from his. He cupped her cheek in his hand and drew her in the rest of the way. She let their lips meet, let the kiss erase everything in her mind.

She was dimly aware that Jake's dad was still sitting right next to them, but she didn't care. She didn't have to care about anything anymore.

* * *

Becca's phone sat in front of her on her desk, next to her

keyboard. She picked it up, stared at it for a moment, put it down again. She ran her fingers along the strip of paper in her hand, now soft and wrinkled from two days of this. She stared at the numbers until her eyes started to cross.

Jake had given her what she wanted. A way out of her helplessness, out of her restlessness. A way to do something. She should have called as soon as she had gotten home from the playground on Friday.

She picked up the phone again. Dialed the first digit.

Surveillance wasn't listening to her calls. They wouldn't waste their time listening in on someone who hadn't done anything suspicious—and anyway, they wouldn't dare put Raleigh Dalcourt's daughter under surveillance.

Probably.

She put the phone down.

She needed Jake to be here. She needed to kiss him again, to drive the fears from her mind for a little while. She hadn't kissed him in two days, not since the day she had watched Anna die. Whenever she went to check on him, she was careful to keep just the right amount of distance between them. She had to figure this out first. She didn't know what it would mean if they kissed again, what the kisses the other day had meant. Maybe she was using him to forget everything that had gone wrong in her life. Maybe he was her own personal Prince Charming and they would go riding off into the sunset and live happily ever after, if Internal didn't take them into that little room and shoot them in the head first.

Maybe she loved him.

She shook her head at the thought, even though there was no one to see her. If she were in love with him, things would be clearer. If she were in love with him, she wouldn't wonder whether she saw him as a way to escape the memories or as her only remaining friend or as something else, something more. Or all of the above. How was she supposed to tell the difference? She needed Heather to help her talk this through, but that wasn't exactly an option anymore.

Maybe she should go back to the playground and check on him. That would be easy. Simple. No matter what she felt or didn't feel, she could go check on him.

Except she couldn't, because she had already gone this morning, to bring food for him and his dad. He didn't want her coming too often, or staying too long; he worried that someone would notice what she was doing. She had told him she hadn't seen her mom since Friday morning and that nobody else would pay attention to how often she left the apartment, but he still didn't think it was safe. Becca wasn't sure she blamed him—after all, how did she know for sure one of her neighbors wasn't watching her out the window, noting down every time she made the trip to the playground?

Maybe she should finish her homework, then.

No, she had finished it all yesterday. It hadn't worked as well as her too-brief times with Jake to block out the image of Anna's death, but it had helped enough that she had done it all at once, losing herself in the tedium for as long as possible.

Becca reached for her phone again. With her hand hovering over it, she stopped. Was there even any point? Even if she did get in touch with these people, what would she be able to do for them?

The phone rang.

Becca nearly fell out of her chair.

Heart pounding, she looked at the display. Heather again. Was this the fifth time Heather had called today, or the sixth?

And that wasn't counting the texts — at least five times as many, all asking her to pick up the phone, to call her back, to meet her somewhere so they could talk. Becca pushed the phone away. She hadn't talked to Heather since their conversation at the playground that night. As far as she was concerned, their friendship was over.

She crumpled and flattened the piece of paper in her hand, like she had done so many times over the past two days. She needed to quit putting this off. This was what she wanted, after all.

The phone stopped ringing.

She picked it up again and—quickly, before she could talk herself out of it again—started dialing.

When she hit the last digit, she stopped.

This was what she wanted. What she needed. She couldn't keep going the way she had been, and this was her only way out.

So why couldn't she make the call?

Someone knocked at her door. Becca jerked and dropped the phone.

"Becca? Are you in there?" Her mom.

"I thought you were still at work." Becca hurriedly cleared the number from her phone. She shoved the phone into her pocket and the slip of paper into her desk drawer. Her mom hadn't even made it home to sleep since the morning Anna had died. Becca hadn't expected to see her at all today, let alone in the middle of the afternoon.

"Public Relations took a bunch of prisoners off our hands this morning, so things have finally calmed down a little. I may even get to sleep in my own bed tonight."

Why had she hidden the phone? Her mom wouldn't be able

to tell what she had been doing with it. Logically, she knew that. Still, she couldn't shake the feeling that even with the phone and paper hidden away, her mom would see right through her.

Since telling her mom to go away wasn't an option, she sat back and waited for her to come in. At least this gave her one more excuse for putting off the call.

Her mom eased the door open. "Is this a good time to talk?"

"Actually, I was trying to get some homework done." She put her hands on her keyboard and tried to look studious.

"I won't take up too much of your time." Her mom walked into the room, closing the door gently behind her, and sat down on the bed. "We need to talk about Anna. We should have talked before now. I shouldn't have left you afterwards the way I did, and I'm sorry. I came back as soon as I could. I've been trying to get home all weekend, but I could barely get a bathroom break."

At the mention of Anna, the loop started playing again behind Becca's eyes. She would have thought that after seeing it so many times, the impact would have faded. It hadn't. She flinched as the gun went off again—the hundredth time? The thousandth?

"Are you doing all right?" Her mom sounded so calm about it. As if what had happened was no more serious than a bad dream.

Becca kept her eyes on the keyboard as she answered. "I watched one of my friends die. What do you think?"

"I'm sorry you had to see that. But you need to understand what's going to happen if you keep going the way you have been." She patted the bed next to her. "Come sit with me."

Becca looked at the space on the bed next to her mom. She wanted to get out of her chair, sit beside her, cry on her shoulder. In the old days, that was what she would have done.

She shook her head. "I'd rather stay here."

The old days were gone.

But her mom still looked like her mom. Why couldn't she look different, now that Becca knew what she really was?

"I don't want you to blame yourself for Anna's death," said her mom. "She would have been executed whether or not you were there. But I do want you to think about what happened to her. If you keep saying the kinds of things you've been saying, you're going to end up right there in one of those cells—" Her voice broke.

That crack in her calm was worse than hearing her talk about Anna's death like it was nothing. Becca didn't want to hear her mom's grief at the thought of losing her. She wanted her mom to sound just as cold about Becca's potential execution as she did about Anna's, so Becca would have one more reason to hate her.

Becca stared out the window so she wouldn't have to look at her mom. Outside, two Enforcers strode through the parking lot. Were they coming home, or on their way to drag away some anonymous dissident destined to die like Anna in one of those tiny rooms?

Becca tried to match her mom's tone, tried to sound like Anna's death didn't matter. Like she didn't see it every time she closed her eyes and sometimes when they were open. "Could we talk about this some other time?" *Or maybe never?* "I'm kind of busy."

Her mom's voice grew sharper. "No. We need to talk about this. We've put it off too long as it is. I never should have let things get this far."

She wanted, needed, to tell her mom everything. How she couldn't get rid of the images. How she sometimes saw not Anna, but Jake, dying in that room... and sometimes she saw herself in Anna's place. How she wished she could go back and undo that conversation where she had lied about Anna, where she had condemned Anna to death.

How much it had scared her to see her mom looking down at Anna's body with blank eyes, and to know that to her this was just a day like any other day.

Deep down, some part of her was still convinced her mom could make it all go away.

"There's nothing to talk about." The Enforcers outside had disappeared from view. "I shouldn't have said those things the other day. I don't even know what I was thinking." But even as she said it, she knew there was no point. That excuse had worked on Heather, but it wouldn't work on her mom.

Her mom reached out and grabbed the arm of Becca's chair. She spun the chair around to face her. "That's not enough this time. I explained the confessions to you; I thought that was the end of this. I thought..." Her voice trailed off. Were those tears glinting at the corners of her eyes? Becca couldn't remember ever seeing her mom cry.

Becca started to speak—but she didn't have anything to say. She had no way to convince her mom she wasn't a dissident. The damage had been done.

"I know things haven't been the same between us lately," said her mom. "But I still know you. You're still Becca. I spend every day with dissidents; I know what they're like. You're not one of them."

And what made Becca so different? The fact that her mom

didn't want her to die? Becca held back the angry words, said nothing, tried to keep her face blank. Was this what their relationship was going to be for the rest of her life?

Why was she still upset at the thought of losing her closeness with her mom? She knew what her mom was like now.

Her mom stretched her arm across the gap and took Becca's hand. The familiar roughness of her skin reminded Becca of all the other times she'd felt that hand around hers, all the times her mom had comforted her when she felt like the world was ending. She needed that now, needed her mom's soothing voice and sensible answers. She needed her mom to hold her and stroke her hair and tell her everything would be all right.

She knew she should pull her hand away. Her mom had blood on her hands—what had she been doing at work all weekend that had kept her too busy to come home? How many dissidents had died? Instead, Becca clutched her mom's hand as she fought the urge to scream about all the things her mom had done. As she fought the urge to break down in tears and admit how afraid she was.

"You need to remember who you are," her mom continued. "That person who said those things the other night about how the country would be better off if the dissidents took over… that isn't you."

"And what about you?" The words left Becca's mouth before she could stop them. "I didn't think you could make people confess to things they hadn't done because you thought they'd be more *useful* that way. I didn't think you could watch somebody die like it was nothing."

Her mom gripped her hand harder. "We've talked about

this. You said you understood. You know why I do what I do."

"But how do you do it? How can you spend your days doing… whatever you do down there…" She shied away from the visions her mind supplied, tried to push away the thought of Anna lying dead on the concrete floor. "…and then come home and talk to me like it doesn't mean anything?"

Her mom frowned and tilted her head. "Did you hear something?"

"Don't change the subject. I want to know. How do you do it?" Suddenly this answer—how her mom could do what she did and still be the person Becca had always known—seemed like the most important thing in the world. But Becca didn't know which she wanted to hear—that both people could coexist in the same body, or that the mother she had grown up with had been an illusion.

Her mom put her finger to her lips.

Were those footsteps?

A door slammed, too loud to be anywhere but inside the apartment.

Becca knew what it meant to hear footsteps that weren't supposed to be there, to hear your door open when nobody else had the key. Everybody knew what that meant.

But her mom had said she wouldn't turn her in. Heather had said she wouldn't turn her in. And it was two in the afternoon. Enforcement took you away in the middle of the night; everyone knew that. It had to be something else. It had to be.

The footsteps were getting closer.

Her mom didn't say anything. She didn't move. But Becca saw her own fear reflected on her face.

The bedroom door opened.

They walked inside. The Enforcers she had seen out in the parking lot a moment ago. She had the answer to her question now. They weren't on their way home. They were here for a dissident. They were here for her.

She couldn't move.

She couldn't breathe.

She didn't understand the things her mom was screaming. It all blended together into a nonsensical jumble. But she could feel her mom's grip on her hand getting tighter and tighter, until the Enforcers pulled them apart.

chapter fifteen

"I'm Raleigh Dalcourt's daughter," she repeated again and again as the Enforcers shoved her through the same side door she had walked through with her mom just two days ago. She tried to keep her voice from shaking, tried to keep her cuffed hands from shaking, tried to keep her legs from collapsing underneath her. "You can't do this."

She had never seen her mom lose control like that before. Even in her arguments with Becca's dad, Becca had never heard her yell. But when Enforcement had come, she had screamed as they had handcuffed Becca and propelled her, too stunned to fight, out the door. First threats that Becca, in her numb state, couldn't understand; then, as the door had closed behind them, a wordless scream that made goosebumps rise all over Becca's body.

The Enforcers hadn't stopped then, and they didn't now.

Still, Becca hung on to the hope that they didn't know. That they thought her mom was just one of many anonymous Internal employees. Once they found out otherwise, they would have to let her go. Hadn't her name gotten her in to see Heather on that horrible night?

The door closed, shutting out her last glimpse of the afternoon sun.

She might never see the sun again.

They maneuvered her into the elevator like a piece of luggage. Inside the elevator, they stood to either side of her, not moving, not speaking.

"I'm Raleigh Dalcourt's daughter," she repeated through her tears. "She works here." The elevator opened onto the maze of hallways underneath 117. The light seemed dimmer now, and the echoes of their footsteps twice as loud. Each of the Enforcers held one of her arms, to keep her from running—where would she go?—and to hurry her along. She stumbled as she tried to keep up; her uneven steps broke the pattern of the echoes.

"She made 117 the best processing center in the country." She hated when other people talked about her mom like this; now she wove the words around her like armor. "She turned this nothing town into someplace the whole country knows about. You wouldn't have jobs if it weren't for her."

Her desperate words rang through the halls. Still, the Enforcers acted like they hadn't heard. They kept going, down one hallway and then another, taking Becca further from the real world with every step.

She didn't know how long they walked before stopping in front of one of the doors. A mix of tears and salty mucus dripped down her face; with her hands cuffed behind her, she couldn't wipe it away. "She's going to come for me," she said as they opened the door. She sounded like Heather had when she had called that night. She could hardly understand herself.

One of the Enforcers shoved her against the wall; the other removed her handcuffs with rough efficiency. Before she could think of taking advantage of her hands' freedom, the one who had taken off the handcuffs pushed her through the door and closed it behind her. The click of the door as it locked had a horrible finality to it.

"She's going to come for me," she repeated to no one.

The cell looked just like the room where Anna had died, except for the metal cot against the far wall. Everything was gray—the walls, the floors, the bed's threadbare sheets. In the corner of the ceiling, a camera watched her. Its tiny red light was the only spot of color in the room. She took a step forward, and although it might have been her imagination, she thought she saw the camera swivel to follow her.

She couldn't stop shaking.

With one hand against the wall, she stumbled to the bed. The metal frame squealed underneath her as she sat down on the rock-hard mattress.

How many dissidents had sat on this bed before her? How long had they stayed in this cell before they died?

How long did Becca have before...

No. She's going to come for me.

A faded bloodstain on the floor caught her eye. It seemed to grow as she looked at it.

She brought her eyes to the ceiling instead—to the camera that, even though she had moved, was still pointed directly at her. "I'm Raleigh Dalcourt's daughter," she told the camera, praying that someone on the other end would hear. "You have to get me out of here." Her voice dropped to a whisper as the last of her strength drained out of her. "Please get me out of here."

Nobody came.

Her shaking got worse.

Even now that she was here, now that it had really happened, it didn't feel possible. She kept waiting to wake up, to come back to reality.

She didn't wake up.

And still nobody came.

She paced back and forth and heard the camera hum as it swiveled to follow her; she sat on the bed and watched the stain on the floor grow. She slept a little, and drifted in and out of nightmares indistinguishable from her reality. When she woke up, it took her a moment to realize this wasn't just another dream.

Her stomach was growling. She felt weak with thirst. She waited for food and water—they had to give her something eventually, they couldn't just let her die in here—but it didn't come.

Nobody came.

She had run out of tears. Her eyes felt like they had been rubbed with sandpaper. Her throat burned with thirst; her tongue kept sticking to the roof of her mouth. Every part of her body ached—whether from sleeping on the hard mattress or from the constant trembling, she didn't know.

She lay down again. Maybe this time, if she managed to fall asleep, she wouldn't dream. Maybe for a while she could turn her mind off and forget where she was.

* * *

Becca drifted from one half-dream to another. The lights blazed through her eyelids into her brain. She got up, paced the room, lay down again, sat and stared at nothing, until she wasn't sure whether she was awake or asleep.

Her mother came. She called Becca a dissident, and Becca couldn't speak. She took a gun from her belt and aimed it at Becca, and Becca couldn't move. Her eyes were cold as she pulled the trigger. Becca woke wiping away tears that weren't there. She had no water left for tears.

Her stomach was twisted in on itself, trying to devour itself. She felt shriveled. Empty. Her tongue was swollen in her parched mouth.

The door opened.

Becca jerked up from the bed as a man ducked through the doorway. She rubbed her eyes and looked again. He hadn't disappeared. And he seemed brighter than the vision of her mom. More solid.

She recognized him. He was the one she and her mom had talked to the other day.

The one who had killed Anna.

She fought back her initial fear and revulsion. She had seen the way he had looked at her mom, how eager he had been to help her. If her mom couldn't come herself, maybe she had sent him to get her out.

She got to her feet, then steadied herself against the wall as her legs threatened to give out under her. "Did my mom send you?" The words scratched against her throat like tiny nails.

A flicker of emotion crossed his face, too fast for her to read. "I need you to come with me."

Her mom had to have sent him. He just couldn't say it here, because... because of the camera. Or because her mom wanted to keep her scared for a little while longer, to teach her a lesson.

His face was expressionless.

His height no longer made him look awkward; he loomed over her as he took a step closer. He held out a pair of handcuffs. "You'll have to be secured."

Maybe her mom had arranged this whole thing. Maybe she thought watching Anna die wasn't enough to keep Becca from turning into a dissident. Her screams as the Enforcers had led Becca out the door... all part of the act.

Wordlessly, Eli pulled Becca's arms behind her back and fastened the handcuffs around her wrists. She let him. It would only be for a few minutes, only until he brought her to her mom.

He took hold of her arm the way the Enforcers had.

"I'm sorry it has to happen this way," he said softly as he led her out the door.

* * *

Becca expected another room like her cell, like the room where Eli had shot Anna. Or maybe something bigger, with a single chair in the center and torture implements laid out in neat rows along a metal table.

She didn't expect anything like what she saw when he opened the door and motioned her inside.

Unlike everything else she had seen on the underground levels, this room didn't have even a hint of gray. The walls, though still noticeably rough concrete, had been painted a warm tan. The carpet was the soothing blue of the ocean, the color of Becca's bedroom walls at home. A wooden desk, big enough that Becca wasn't sure how it could have made it through the door, took up most of the space in the small room, and a chair made from the same dark wood sat to either side.

A camera, identical to the one in her cell, watched her from the corner.

Becca stepped into the room. Eli unlocked the handcuffs and gestured to the chair nearest her. "Sit down."

She almost fell crossing the short distance to the chair. Eli made his way around the desk and folded himself into the chair opposite her.

There was a glass of water on the desk, next to a small stack of papers. Once Becca spotted it, she couldn't see anything else. She imagined reaching across the desk and grabbing it, feeling the cold on her tongue as she poured the liquid down her throat. Her hand twitched.

Eli pushed the glass across the desk. "Have as much as you want."

Her hand felt weak and trembly as she closed her fingers around the glass. She gingerly brought it to her lips, afraid she would drop it. She took a small sip first, then gulped faster until the glass was empty. The coolness of the water spread from her stomach out through the rest of her body. Not enough. But she felt a little better.

She glanced at the closed door. Any minute now, and her mom would walk in, ready to take her home. Any minute now...

The door stayed closed.

Her mom wasn't coming.

Why had she even bothered trying to fool herself? If her mom had been able to save her, she would have stopped Enforcement from taking her in the first place. If anyone cared whose daughter she was, they would have released her by now.

Her breaths grew ragged as the truth closed in on her. There would be no rescue. They would get whatever confession they needed from her, and then they would kill her just like Anna.

"You have to let me go," she told Eli anyway. She tried to sound unafraid, but her voice, weak and rough from crying, broke on the first word. "Before my mom finds out I'm here." Her words echoed with the hollowness of her threat. Her mom already knew she was here.

"I wish you didn't have to be here." His regret sounded genuine. Not that that meant anything. "Raleigh Dalcourt is my role model. I respect her more than anyone else I've ever met." He paused for a moment, straightening the papers on the desk. "But as much as she matters to me, our purpose here matters more. Nothing can get in the way of that purpose. She taught me that."

"I haven't done anything." Why had she bothered to say it? She knew it didn't matter what she had or hadn't done.

"I want this to be over just as much as you do. I want to get you back home with your mother where you belong." Eli rested his arms on the desk and leaned toward her. "We can do that. Nothing you've done is that serious. It's obvious you're not a threat to society."

Becca tensed, wanting so badly to believe him, waiting for the catch.

"All you have to do," he said, "is tell us where to find your friend Jake."

Jake. Of course. That was why they had brought her here. Somehow they had found out about her warning.

Jake, hiding with his dad in the playhouse. Had he started wondering yet why she hadn't come to bring him more food?

What would happen to him if she never got out of here?

Eli had said she could go home.

All she had to do was give him Jake. Trade Jake's life, and his dad's, for hers.

Maybe he was lying. She knew all about Internal's lies. She wanted to believe he was lying; that was easier than wondering whose life was worth more.

Eli flipped through the papers on his desk until he found what he was looking for. "We know you've been helping him hide from Enforcement. We heard your phone call warning him."

She should have expected it. Should have known better than to think she could do something like this—helping a dissident evade Internal, dissident activity by any definition—without ending up right where she was now.

Becca didn't say anything. Was there any point in trying to pretend she hadn't helped Jake? And yet she couldn't bring herself to say she had done it, couldn't admit to dissident activity in this of all places.

"Did Jake approach you first," Eli asked, "or was it one of the teachers?"

Becca blinked. "What?"

"Who was it that recruited you? Was it Jake, or the teacher who told you to warn him and find him a place to hide?"

The teacher thing, Internal's invented conspiracy. He wanted to weave her into it. Make her useful. Just like her mom had said.

"There isn't—" She almost told him there had never been any conspiracy, almost admitted she knew what Internal had been doing. She stopped herself just in time. If they knew her mom had betrayed Internal's secrets by telling her...

So what if they knew? Her mom hadn't gotten her out of here. Why should Becca protect her?

But she didn't finish her sentence.

She started over. "He didn't recruit me into anything. Nobody did."

"Please, Becca. I just want to get you out of this place. You know what will happen to you if you stay here."

She didn't answer.

"You don't have to worry about how it will reflect on you. With a mother like yours, I know you would never have ended up in a position like this if there weren't some very persuasive people behind it. I understand. Just tell me what Jake and the others have been telling you, and who told you to protect him."

"You said all I had to do was tell you where Jake was." Not that it mattered; she wouldn't have told him anyway. She wouldn't have traded Jake's life and his dad's for hers. Right?

Right?

"That would be a good start," he said. "But finding one dissident isn't going to help us very much, especially since he's probably an innocent victim like you. We need to find the people responsible for dragging kids like you into this. Maybe it wasn't even anybody at your school. Maybe this has reached further than we suspected."

He wouldn't let her go. No matter what she told him, no matter who she accused. He would add it to their collection of false confessions and use it to condemn more innocent people. Public Relations would take advantage of the fact that she was Raleigh Dalcourt's daughter to prove that the dissidents could corrupt anyone. And she would die in the room where Anna had died, or on TV for everyone in the country to watch.

He wouldn't let her go. It was a lie.

Wasn't it?

Eli sighed. "This is silly, Becca. Why are you protecting these people, after what they've gotten you into? Why are you protecting Jake, when he's the reason you're here in the first place?"

How did she know it was a lie? Her mom had even told her Internal let people go sometimes if they weren't a threat to society. Eli had said she wasn't a threat. Maybe she didn't have to end up like Anna. Maybe she could walk out of this place and forget any of this had ever happened.

She could say Jake's dad had gotten her involved in whatever this was supposed to be. Eli had said it didn't have to be a teacher, after all. That way she wouldn't have to condemn anybody else—Jake's dad would end up here anyway if she told Eli where Jake was.

No. What was she thinking? How could she even consider killing them for the sake of her own possible freedom? The cost was too high.

Anna wouldn't have been here, wouldn't have died here, if not for Becca's lie. Nobody else would die because of her.

"All I did was call him," she answered. "I don't know where he went. And nobody recruited me into anything."

So easy, too easy, to say the words that determined the way her life would end.

She couldn't tell whether the sadness in his eyes was real or as much of a lie as everything he had said about the conspiracy. "In that case, I guess I don't have a choice."

She had thought she would start crying again. She didn't. She sat perfectly still, trying not to imagine what was coming.

Eli walked over to her. "Give me your hands."

She held her arms out to him; he refastened the handcuffs. He guided her out of the chair and toward the door, one slow step at a time.

As he reached for the door, it flew open.

Becca's mom stood in the doorway.

chapter sixteen

Becca's mom blocked the door, wild-eyed, hair spilling out of her untidy braid. "I'm here to take my daughter home."

Becca pulled away from Eli and rushed into her mom's arms. It didn't matter what her mom had done, or how she had lied. All that mattered was that she was here, and she was going to get Becca out of this place. She was going to save Becca's life.

Her mom wrapped her arms around her, a noise like a sob escaping her throat. Becca would have clutched her mom just as hard if not for the handcuffs. Tears of relief prickled at the corners of her eyes.

Her mom smelled like day-old sweat. Becca didn't care.

"I can't let her go," said Eli from behind her. "I'm sorry, Raleigh."

"I talked to the directors." Becca felt the heat of her mom's breath against her hair as she spoke. "It took me two days, but I got them to agree. She's free to go." She let go of Becca with one arm to pull something out of her bag. "The forms are right here."

Two days? Had Becca really been here that long? How long had she waited in that cell?

"You need to think about this, Raleigh. What will happen to you if you let a dissident go free? It could mean the end of your career, or worse. You'd probably be investigated."

Her mom's voice turned glacial; even though it wasn't directed at her, Becca shivered. "What are you accusing me of?"

"I know you're not a dissident," he said hastily. "I understand. You just want to keep your daughter safe. But you have to think about how it will look."

Her mom's voice didn't warm up. "My daughter is not a dissident."

"There's evidence against her," Eli persisted.

Her mom's arms tightened around her. "I've seen your evidence. I think it's ridiculous, and the directors agree."

Eli made a disapproving noise. "If you're sure you want to do this, and you've convinced the directors to go along with it, there's nothing I can do to stop you. But you still have a chance to change your mind. If you think it through—"

Her mom cut him off. "I'm not leaving this room without her." Her tone made the way Jake had threatened Laine sound like the mewling of a kitten by comparison.

Eli sighed. "Like I said, I can't stop you."

Her mom released her slowly, like she had to pry her own arms away. Eli fiddled with Becca's handcuffs until they slid off her wrists. She rubbed her wrists and swayed on her feet. The world wobbled around her.

Her mom put an arm around her shoulder. "Let's get out of here."

* * *

Leaving 117 felt like being reborn.

As her mom guided her out the door and across the parking lot, the sun shone down on her as brightly as it had yesterday—no, two days ago—when the Enforcers had brought her here. She could almost believe that no time had gone by at all, that her time on the underground levels had been nothing more than a bad dream.

The world jolted; Becca stumbled over nothing. The rows of cars in front of her blurred.

Her mom dug through her bag and pulled out a water bottle. She handed it to Becca. "Drink this."

Becca unscrewed the cap on her second try. She greedily gulped down half the bottle, then choked as the liquid turned out to be thick and syrupy-sweet. Her stomach growled, caught between nausea and renewed hunger. Hunger won; she drained the bottle as she climbed into the car.

It took her mom two tries to turn the key in the ignition with her shaking fingers. "Tell me they were wrong about you," she said in a voice on the edge of tears, a voice Becca had never heard from her before. "Tell me you didn't help that dissident hide."

Becca stared out the window at Processing 117 as the car began to move. It looked the same as it always had. Everything looked the same.

I almost died in there.

She couldn't stop shivering. She wrapped her arms around herself, even though she wasn't cold. Why couldn't she stop shivering? She was safe now.

"Please." Her mom weaved out of the parking lot, and jerked the steering wheel to the left seconds before she would have slammed into a parked car. "Tell me you didn't do it."

Out of the parking lot. Away from 117. Becca rested her head against the car window and closed her eyes, overcome by a wave of dizziness. She stammered out a denial through her chattering teeth. "I... I d-didn't do anything. I didn't even know Internal was... was after him." Her mom would see through her; her mom always saw through her. Would she turn around and give Becca back to Eli when she realized Becca was guilty after all?

"You called him the morning Enforcement came for him. When they got to his house, he was gone."

Becca opened her eyes, then quickly closed them again. The world was going by too fast. "I c-called him to hang out. That's... that's all." It didn't matter what she said. Her mom would figure out the truth, and then she would bring Becca back to that cell...

"So you don't know where he is." The car swerved sharply to the side. Becca opened her eyes in time to see them swing back into the right lane, narrowly avoiding a head-on collision.

"N-no." Jake had been waiting for two days. Did he suspect what had happened to her?

"I knew you couldn't do something like that." Her mom tightened her fingers around the steering wheel like she was trying to choke the life out of it. "You've said some misguided things lately, but that doesn't mean you would help a dissident hide from Internal. Even if he is a friend of yours." She paused. "You're certain you don't know where he is?"

"I d-didn't even know... know he was a dissident. I thought you w-were wrong about him." She waited for her mom to confront her, to expose her lie.

"I'm sorry for doubting you." Her mom's death grip on the steering wheel loosened a tiny bit. "But I had to hear it from you."

Her mom hadn't seen through her lie. She was safe.

Alive. Safe. Free.

She still couldn't stop shivering.

"I did everything I could to get you out of there," said her mom as they got closer to the apartment. "I'm sorry it took as long as it did."

Looking more closely at her mom's face, Becca saw the dark circles under her eyes, and the new wrinkles that made her look as if she had aged ten years overnight. "Are you r-really going to... to b-be investigated?"

"Maybe," said her mom. "But they won't find anything. Anyway, it doesn't matter. What matters is that I got you out of there."

Why was she worried about her mom's safety, anyway? Had she forgotten what her mom had done? What she did every day?

But she had saved Becca's life. And even if she hadn't, she was still her mom. Becca imagined the Enforcers handcuffing her mom instead of her, pushing her mom ahead of them out the door while Becca stood by helplessly. No matter what she thought of her mom, Becca would have been the one screaming without words, the one searching for any possible way to save her.

"Th-thank you," said Becca. "For... for saving me. And p-putting yourself in danger to do it."

Her mom pulled into the parking lot of their building. "There was no other option. I couldn't leave you there."

Even if I really did help Jake?

She didn't ask. She thought she knew the answer, anyway. Somewhere deep down, her mom had to at least suspect what Becca was. What she had done.

And she had saved her anyway.

"Is there any chance they'll... they'll arrest me again?" Becca asked.

The car slid into their parking space. "No. They had no meaningful evidence against you. I've made that clear to them." Her mom yanked the key out of the ignition and swung her car door open.

Not that it matters whether they have evidence or not. Becca kept her mouth shut as she fumbled with her seatbelt. She wasn't quite as dizzy anymore. Whatever her mom had given her had helped.

Her mom kept talking as she climbed out of the car. "All they had was that phone call and what that dissident friend of yours said."

Becca froze halfway through taking off her seatbelt. "Heather? Heather turned me in?"

"This is how far she's willing to go to keep suspicion off herself. I did warn you about her. She isn't someone you want to associate with."

Heather had turned her in.

It's a lie. Just another lie.

But Becca didn't know who was lying—her mother, or

Heather.

* * *

For once, Becca's mom was home when Becca woke up. Becca got ready for school as her mom hovered; she choked down the toast her mom made for her; she assured her that she was okay, of course she was okay. They left the apartment together, Becca's forced smile growing more and more strained under her mom's watchful eyes.

Becca stood at the front of the parking lot, where the bus would pick her up. She and Heather used to wait for the bus here together; now, with Heather gone, Becca was the only high-school student in the building who took the bus to school. Her mom passed her in her car, on her way to 117 to do to other dissidents what she had saved Becca from. Becca watched the car until it was out of sight. She waited an extra couple of minutes just to be safe. Then she started out of the parking lot, toward the playground.

She hadn't been able to sneak away to see Jake yesterday after she got home; her mom had kept too close an eye on her. He and his dad had been waiting for three days now. Did they think she wasn't coming back? Did they think it was only a matter of time now before Internal came for them?

The food she had left them had probably run out by now. She hadn't been able to grab anything this morning, but she could come back with food later. Right now the most important thing was to let them know that she was alive, and that she hadn't forgotten them.

The apartment building receded into the distance behind her. Somebody might have watched her leave, and wondered why she was going to the playground so often all of a sudden and why she was skipping school to do it. She glanced back at the building, squinting to see if she could spot any faces in the windows. She was too far away to tell, but she thought she might have seen one of the curtains move.

When she had warned Jake, she hadn't thought about anything but keeping him safe from the immediate threat. She should have thought further, should have understood that the threat didn't end there. Internal was looking for him, and eventually they would find him. She didn't just need to bring food; she needed to warn him that he had to run. Leave town with his dad as soon as possible. They would still be in danger, but it would give them the best chance of survival.

She would never see him again. But he would be safe from Internal. Safer, at least.

She tried not to think about how alone she would be once he was gone.

She heard something. Footsteps? She spun around, but saw only the parking lot where she was supposed to be waiting for the bus.

It was probably for the best that she wasn't going to school; everybody had to know about her arrest by now. And this time Jake wouldn't be around to protect her.

And then there was Heather. How was she supposed to face Heather?

When Becca didn't show up at school, would the Monitors report it? Would Internal assume she was guilty after all, and that she had run before they could discover their mistake?

She slowed down as she got closer to the playground. She looked behind her again. Still nobody there. Why did she feel like someone was watching her?

If anyone saw her, if anyone found out what she was doing, she would end up right back in 117 again, and this time her mom wouldn't be able to save her.

She stopped.

Jake needs me.

What would have happened to her in 117 if her mom hadn't come through that door?

I almost died in there.

She tried to force her legs forward. She had promised herself that no one else would die because of her. What if Jake and his dad died because she had abandoned them?

Her feet were glued to the pavement.

I almost died.

Anyone passing by would be able to see her standing by the side of the road like this. Anyone would be able to guess what she was doing. Helping a dissident. Dissident activity.

A car roared up behind her; her legs nearly buckled. The car sped past and disappeared into the distance. Not Enforcement after all. She gulped in a lungful of air. Her hands shook.

Jake was waiting for her. How long before Internal found him?

With one last look toward the playground, Becca turned and bolted back to the parking lot.

Coward.

chapter seventeen

Becca sleepwalked through her classes. She didn't hear a single word her teachers said; she only heard the word that followed her through the halls the way it used to circle through her mind. *Dissident.*

Most people kept their distance. A few approached her, hanging back as if she might bite. They asked if it was true that Internal had arrested her, that she had helped a dissident escape from 117, that she had been seconds from execution before her mom had forced Internal to let her go. The threats hadn't started yet, but it was only a matter of time.

As she entered the cafeteria, the roar of conversation quieted. All through the room, heads pointed in her direction. The word echoed off the walls like her footsteps had echoed through the underground levels. *Dissident, dissident, dissident...*

Becca backed up. She would spend lunch somewhere else. Anywhere else. She hadn't brought anything to eat, but right now just the smell of the cafeteria's stale pizza was more than her stomach could handle.

At the left-hand table near the door, where the political kids sat, somebody stood up. Becca took another step back; maybe if she left the cafeteria fast enough her would-be tormentor wouldn't follow.

Wait. That was Heather.

One more reason to get out of there. Becca turned around and grabbed blindly for the door.

Heather reached her just as her fingers closed around the door handle. She threw her arms around Becca like a snake trying to strangle its prey. No... like the way her mom had held her in 117. This wasn't an attack; it was a hug.

"I'm so glad you're okay," Heather whispered.

Becca pulled away. She held Heather at arm's length, studied her face for signs that her mom had been telling the truth. Heather's relief seemed real... but how could she tell? How could she tell about anyone anymore?

"Is it true? Did you turn me in?" She didn't care who heard her ask. If people thought Heather had reported her, it would just make Heather look better, and Becca should want that, right? She had tried so hard to help Heather; why stop now?

"No! Why would you even think that?" Heather's denial came a second too late; she looked away as she said it.

"You did. You turned me in." She said it so softly she almost couldn't hear herself. She didn't want to hear herself say it. Didn't want to face the truth.

"I didn't do it," said Heather, pleading now.

"Stop lying to me!" Now her voice was too loud, almost

yelling. Nearby conversations quieted again as people listened. She tried to lower her voice. "Why can't you just tell me the truth?"

"Just let me explain, okay? Please." Heather grabbed Becca's hand and tugged her toward the door. Becca let Heather lead her out into the hall. Even listening to Heather explain her betrayal sounded like a better prospect than staying in the cafeteria with all those hostile eyes on her.

Once the door had closed behind them, Heather let go of Becca's hand. Becca thought about running as fast as she could down the empty hallway, maybe even out the front entrance and all the way home, and leaving Heather here alone with her explanation unspoken. But a part of her wanted to hear it, to know how Heather could have turned on her so thoroughly. She matched Heather's pace as they wandered.

"I didn't mean to do it," said Heather quietly.

Becca didn't look at Heather; she looked everywhere else so she wouldn't have to. The lights seemed too bright, the halls too wide, after the dim narrow maze of the underground levels. "What did you do, call them by accident?"

"They came to my house. Two of them. It was a couple of days after I... you know. After I reported Jake." She cringed away from Becca a little as she said it.

Becca didn't respond.

"They thought I had warned Jake and his dad. They said I was doing what my parents had done—trying to get Internal to trust me while I secretly worked against them. They said that's why I joined the Monitors, and why I turned Jake in."

"So you told them I must have warned him." Heather had offered Becca up as a sacrifice, as though their years of friendship meant nothing. *Coward.* Becca wanted to throw the word in her face.

Was Becca any better? She had abandoned Jake and his dad.

"I didn't understand what I had done until it was too late." Heather's steps slowed. "I tried to tell you, after. You have to believe me."

All those unanswered phone calls. Maybe Heather really had tried to warn her.

And what if Becca had died in there? Would Heather's last-minute change of heart have mattered then?

Heather stopped; so did Becca. Heather didn't say anything else. She looked at Becca, waiting.

Becca knew what Heather wanted. She wanted Becca to forgive her, to say she understood. To say it was okay that she had almost died because her best friend had only cared about saving herself.

She couldn't give Heather what she wanted. But she couldn't walk away, either. Hadn't she almost made the same decision as Heather? Hadn't she at least considered it, sitting in that room in 117?

And what about now? What about Jake, hiding in the playhouse, waiting for her?

Coward.

She didn't know anymore whether she meant Heather or herself.

Heather is the reason Jake is there in the first place, Becca reminded herself. *If she hadn't turned him in, he'd be here at school right now.*

That reminder made the situation simpler. Maybe Becca had been tempted to sacrifice Jake after her arrest, but she would never have coldly handed him over to Internal the way Heather had. Heather wasn't just a coward; she had become something worse.

She turned the thought around in her head, let it drive out all the others, until it tipped the balance and allowed her to walk down the hall alone, leaving Heather behind.

* * *

Becca tossed her backpack onto the living room floor. She was about to head to her bedroom when she heard a soft thump from the kitchen. She stopped moving, held her suddenly-quivering body in place with one foot raised mid-step. As she listened, it happened again. The sound of a drawer closing, then footsteps. Someone was here. *Internal*.

They hadn't see her yet, but they must have heard the door open and close. Could she make it out of the apartment before they caught up with her? But even if she did, they would come after her, and she couldn't outrun—

Her mom stepped out of the kitchen.

Becca let her foot drop to the floor, let the air hiss out of her lungs. "It's you."

"I came home early. I wanted to make sure you were all right." Her mom frowned as she scrutinized Becca. "What happened?"

"Nothing. I thought you were Internal." Becca's legs threatened to give out as her adrenaline abruptly receded. She rested her back against the door, trying to look casual, like it was no big deal. "How did you manage to leave work so early? It's the middle of the afternoon."

"Someone else can handle my dissidents today. Or they can sit in their cells a little longer. Being here for you is more important."

Becca wished her mom had stayed at work until after midnight again instead. Having her around wasn't going to help anything. Not when every time Becca looked at her she thought about Jake's mom and Heather's parents and Anna and everything her job meant. Not when every second that went by was another opportunity for her mom to discover that Becca wasn't innocent after all.

Except that seeing her mom in front of her, knowing she was here, did make it a little easier for Becca to breathe. Why did her mom's presence still comfort her, even now that Becca knew what she was?

Every time she talked to her mom lately, she ended up seeing double. The torturer. Her mother. One and the same, and yet how could they be?

"You never got a chance to answer my question," said Becca.

"What question?" Her mom stepped closer. Becca didn't know whether she wanted to back up against the door as far as she could or rush into her mom's arms and tell her all about her miserable day.

"How you... do what you do."

Her mom was silent for a moment. Was she remembering the same thing as Becca? Becca asking the question, then the sound of footsteps, and then...

Her mom spoke, chasing the memory from Becca's mind. "I do what I do because I have to."

Becca shook her head. "That's not true. You didn't have to get a job in Processing. You didn't have to get a job with Internal at all. You chose this—and every morning you choose to stay there for another day. So how do you do it? How do you keep going back?" She couldn't find the right words to ask what she really wanted to know—how her mom could go back there every day and still be the mother Becca had grown up with.

"A lot of people don't stay," said her mom. "They last a few months, or a year, and then they transfer someplace else. Surveillance, maybe, or Investigation... sometimes they leave Internal altogether." She paused. "I admit I've had moments when the idea seemed very tempting. Processing is... not an easy place to work. But what would happen if everybody walked away? Without Processing, there would be no point to Surveillance or Investigation or any of the rest. So I stand by what I said—I do it because I have to."

"That's *why* you stay," said Becca. "But *how* do you do it? You're not..." She didn't know how to finish the sentence, didn't know how to put her thoughts into words.

"I choose to," her mom answered. "It's that simple."

"You could say that about anything. You could say that if you quit tomorrow to become a clown." Her mom's answer was too easy, and explained too little. It didn't give Becca what she was looking for.

Her mom's face darkened. "Do you think I take this choice that lightly? Do you think it matters that little to me? If that were the case, I would have left Processing a long time ago." She wrapped her arms around her chest. "I lost your father because I wouldn't leave Processing. And I've given up more than my marriage. People know how important Processing is, and they're always quick to tell me how much they admire what I've done for 117 and for Internal... but they never want to get too close. Have you ever wondered why you're the closest friend I have?" She drew in a shaky breath. "And every day when I look at the dissidents in those cells, I have to

- 223 -

remind myself all over again what they are, so that I can do what needs to be done."

In all their conversations, over all these years, her mom had never hinted at any of this.

"But I stay. I stay because I will not be someone who abandons my principles as soon as they become inconvenient. I will not be someone who says that certain things have to be done... as long as *somebody else* does them." Her mom crossed the remaining distance to Becca and took Becca's face in her hands. "This is the most important thing I can teach you. Living by your principles will always be the harder path. But you have to do it anyway. You have to do what's right no matter how hard it gets, or one day you'll find out you've become somebody you can't live with."

A chill spread through Becca's body. A horrible recognition that drove all her thoughts about her mom's job out of her mind.

Jake, waiting in the playground. Abandoned.

Could she live with herself if she left him there?

Her mom let her hands fall to her sides. "I know how hard it is. It's easier to hate the people who killed your best friend's parents than to understand why their deaths were necessary. It's easier to believe a friend's lies than to accept that he's using you. But you know what's right. And you have to keep reminding yourself of that."

She did know what was right.

And leaving Jake at the playground wasn't it.

Her mom was waiting for a response.

"I've been trying." Becca didn't have to fake sincerity. "But... it's hard."

"I know it is," her mom said gently. "But it's the only way

you're going to get through this."

* * *

Becca tiptoed out of her bedroom. She winced as the floor creaked under her feet. Her mom's door stood slightly open; through it Becca saw her mom's arm hanging off the bed, heard the slow rhythmic sound of her breathing.

Her mom mumbled something incoherent. Becca stopped, waiting to hear her name or a question about what she was doing up so late. Instead the mattress squeaked as her mom's breathing settled back into its regular pattern.

Becca crept past her door, through the hallway, into the living room. She slipped her shoes on and picked up her backpack. Once she had swung the backpack onto her back, she opened the door inch by inch, cringing at every squeal of the hinges. She stood in the doorway, listening for any hint that the noise might have woken her mom.

If her mom woke up, she couldn't leave.

Nothing. Her mom was still asleep.

She told herself she was relieved.

She stepped out of the apartment and closed the door as carefully as she had opened it.

Down the hall. Down the stairs. Trying not to think of who might hear her footsteps and open their doors to see who was wandering around in the middle of the night. Just paranoia. Nobody could hear her from inside their apartments, and if they could, they wouldn't think anything of it. Around here, people came and went at all hours; Becca's mom wasn't the only one who sometimes didn't stumble home from work until six in the morning.

Becca walked outside into the cool night air. The last time she had been out this late, she had been hiding in the playhouse, the way Jake was now.

At least, if he was still there.

He had to still be there.

The thought of Jake forced her forward, away from the building, into the parking lot.

Directly into the path of an Enforcer.

They had been watching her, waiting for her to do something like this. And now that she had confirmed their suspicions, now that they had caught her—

He gave her a wave as he ambled toward the building.

She told her heart to slow down. Just a neighbor on his way home from work, too bleary from his long day to register anything strange about Becca's middle-of-the-night wanderings.

Maybe seeing him had been a warning, a way of telling her to turn around before it was too late

She adjusted her backpack and kept going.

Out of the parking lot, into the shadows. Leaving the light of the parking lot at least meant less chance of being seen. But it also meant she couldn't see who was waiting for her. Anybody could be out there between her and the playground, just waiting for her to get a little closer, for her to prove she was what they thought she was.

She tried to shake off her worries. Nobody was waiting for her. Her mom had said they wouldn't arrest her again. But her fear weighed her down as much as the backpack on her shoulders, making every step slower as she squinted into the darkness.

She had never noticed before just how many steps it took

to get to the playground. How many trees stood between her and her destination, looming over her with their branches stretched out like grasping hands. How many dark places there were in the construction site where someone could lurk without being seen. How many times her heart could beat in the few minutes she spent walking this short stretch of road.

And then she was there, standing in the weeds with the playhouse in front of her. Her feet felt twice as heavy, each step twice as long, as she crossed the playground to where Jake was hiding, where he had to be hiding.

She couldn't hear anything from inside the playhouse.

He had to be in there.

She took a deep breath—but before she could step inside, a dark shape hurtled toward her and threw her to the ground.

chapter eighteen

They had found her. They had been waiting here for her all along. She should have known better than to come back here. Now they would bring her back to 117, and this time her mom wouldn't be able to save her.

She fought blindly, thrashing on her belly like a fish out of water. Where was that noise coming from? Was she screaming? When had she started screaming?

Her attacker pinned her to the grass with the weight of his body. His hands moved up to her neck, crept around to her throat, started squeezing. Her scream turned into a gurgle, then stopped entirely; she gasped for breath, her struggles becoming more frantic.

He would kill her here, or arrest her and bring her back to 117 so she could die there. Either way, she died. They had found her, her release had meant nothing, they had come for her again...

Her lungs burned. She strained for air, but could only pull in a thin stream. Not enough.

The hands around her neck loosened.

She greedily gulped in air, heart pounding, tears springing to her eyes. It didn't matter whether he let her live, it didn't matter, they would kill her in 117 anyway...

"Becca?"

She heard her name from very far away.

Who was calling her?

It didn't matter.

"I'm sorry, Becca. I didn't know it was you. I thought it had to be them, so I panicked. I didn't even think..."

The things the voice was saying didn't make any sense. But it didn't matter; nothing mattered now. She tried to get up, tried to run, but even though her attacker wasn't holding her down anymore—when had he stopped holding her down?—she couldn't make her shaking limbs cooperate. When she tried to push herself off the ground, her arm gave out underneath her, dropping her face-first back down into the weeds.

Even if she managed to get away, he would still come after her. No matter how far she ran, they would find her. They would always find her.

"Becca, it's me. It's Jake."

More meaningless words, reaching her ears from a million miles away.

Her heart was going to explode in her chest. She had to get out of here, had to get away, but she couldn't move...

"Becca. Come back. It's me. It's just me."

They had found her...

They were going to come for her...

He stroked her hair. This time she recognized the touch, didn't flinch, didn't fight him. Jake. Alive, safe, free. Just like her.

For now.

For how long?

Even now that she knew who he was, now that she knew she was safe, she couldn't move, couldn't do anything but lie facedown on the ground and shiver and cry and wait for them to take her.

* * *

She didn't know how long she lay in the grass with Jake's soothing voice in her ears. By the time he led her into the playhouse, she had mostly stopped shaking; her heart had almost slowed down to normal.

The smell of unwashed human overlaid the playhouse's usual moldy odor. Jake's dad sat in the same corner as before, staring off into the distance. Had he moved at all since Becca had left last time? She set her backpack down, then slid to the floor herself, still too weak to be confident that she could stay on her feet.

She opened the backpack and distributed what little food she had managed to smuggle away as she explained in a wobbly voice what had happened. She left out the part about how she had nearly abandoned them; she let Jake think she had only just gotten out of 117. Jake's dad twitched an arm out to grab one of the apples she had brought. He kept his eyes fixed on that same spot in the distance as he ate.

While Becca spoke, Jake wrapped an arm around her shoulders. She tensed at first, then leaned into him. The heat of his body radiated through her, chasing away the cold her fear had left behind. His solid presence was a wall between her and the world. She wished she could hide there forever.

But the world was still out there. She couldn't hide forever, and neither could Jake. That was why she had come here.

"You have to run," she told him. "The longer you stay, the more likely it is that someone will realize you're here. You need to leave while you still have a chance."

Jake shook his head. "Not yet."

"I don't know how long you have before they find you. If you wait too long, it'll be too late." Worries crept into her mind as she spoke. How were they going to run? They had no money and nowhere to go. Even if Jake's dad could take care of himself, they wouldn't have much of a chance.

But if they stayed, they had none.

Jake pulled his arm back to his lap; Becca shivered from the sudden cold. "We're not leaving." His voice was as cold as the air, as cold as the fear he had shielded her from a few short seconds ago.

What had just happened?

"It's not that I want you to leave, if that's what you're thinking. I... I don't want to lose you." Her cheeks heated up at the words, honest as they were. "But if you stay—"

He cut her off. "It's not about you."

"So what is it about?" She pushed herself back, away from him, as she scooted sideways to face him. "What do you think you're going to do? Hide here forever? No matter how small your chances are if you run, they'll be worse if you stay." Her voice filled the tiny playhouse. "They'll kill you. Both of you."

She glanced from Jake to his dad, who hadn't moved. "You said you needed to protect your dad," she said more quietly. "You need to protect him now by getting out of here."

Jake stood up. The sudden movement stirred the dust on the floor, making Becca's nose tickle. "Don't tell me how to protect him."

Becca clambered to her feet. She didn't want him looming over her as she talked. "How are you going to protect him if you stay here?"

"How am I going to protect him if I leave?" Jake glared at some invisible point in the center of the room. For a second he and his dad looked alike, both in their own worlds, staring at something no one else could see. "We have to stay. It's the only way he'll ever be safe."

"That doesn't make any sense." Becca put a hand on his shoulder, trying to bring him back, trying to reassure herself that he was still there. He shook her hand off and backed away.

From the corner, a rough voice spoke. "Maybe she's right."

Becca turned to face Jake's dad. He was still sitting in the exact same position; he wasn't even looking at them. But he had spoken.

"Let me handle this," said Jake. "I know what I'm doing."

"If we stay here, we're not safe." Jake's dad blinked slowly. "You're not safe."

"You think that matters?" Jake shifted restlessly, like he wasn't sure what to do with his body. "We've come this far. I'm not walking away now. I threw away my chance once already. I won't run and lose the opportunity forever."

"The opportunity for what?" Becca asked.

Neither of them looked at her.

"If we stay, we'll die. I'll lose you like I lost them." His dad finally turned his head to look at Jake. His face was full of desperation, the same desperation Becca had seen in him when she had gone to their house that day. "What good will it do to kill her if you die too?"

The rest of his words faded into the background, leaving only two ringing in her ears.

Kill her.

Jake stepped between Becca and his dad. His face twisted between rage and panic.

Becca looked past Jake, directing her question to his dad. "Kill who?"

But she didn't need to hear the answer. She knew it before the name left his lips.

"Raleigh Dalcourt."

chapter nineteen

Becca waited for Jake to deny what his dad had said, to say something—anything—that would make her believe it wasn't true. But looking at him, she knew he wouldn't.

"What do you want me to say?" Jake challenged. "Of course I have to kill her. What else am I supposed to do—keep going on like this, watching him get worse and worse every day, waiting for them to come for us again? It's the only way I can keep him safe. It's the only thing I can do for Mom and Sarra." His voice steadied as he spoke. "I can't undo any of what happened, but I can do this. They'll probably find me and kill me afterwards, but it doesn't matter. She'll be dead. They can't undo that any more than I can bring Mom and Sarra back."

Becca wanted Jake to look like a stranger to her. Like a

killer. But he looked the same as he had when they had first met, the same as he had a few minutes ago when he had comforted her. She couldn't keep looking at him—but she couldn't turn away, either.

She couldn't breathe.

"Please, Jake," said his dad from the corner. "Just forget all this. Run like she told you to."

Jake ignored him.

"Everything between us," Becca forced out. "Everything you did for me. It was just to get to her, wasn't it?"

"No!" He barked the word, a desperate denial. "I didn't expect you to be who you were. I never thought you would be like us. After I knew, all of it was real."

He reached his hand out to her. She recoiled.

The light in his eyes dimmed, but only for a second. "And because you're a dissident," he continued, as if she hadn't just pulled away, "you understand why I have to do this."

Becca gaped at him. "You're talking about killing my mom."

"I'm talking about killing a torturer." Jake's eyes seared into her. "You know what she is."

Reluctantly, Becca nodded.

"And you still think she deserves to live?" Jake demanded.

"She's my mother." It was the only answer she had. It didn't feel like enough.

"And what about my mother?" Jake's voice vibrated against the walls. "What about my sister? What about all the other people she tortures and kills every day?"

Becca had nothing to say, no words she could offer that would erase the truth of what Jake had said. She knew what her mom was. What she had done. What she would continue to do, day after day, because her principles demanded it.

"I know you hate what she does," said Jake. "This is your chance to keep her from hurting anyone else. You don't even have to do anything. Just get me into the apartment, and I'll take care of the rest."

She had to say no. She couldn't let him kill her mom.

The answer stuck in her throat.

She knew what her mom was. With Anna's execution still as vivid behind her eyes as it had been the moment she had witnessed it, she couldn't bring herself to say no. But she couldn't say yes, either.

Jake shook his head in disgust. "You're just like the resistance group Sarra was working with. They wouldn't help me kill her either. All their reasons were nothing but excuses. I know the real reason. You know what needs to be done, but you're not willing to do it yourself." He turned away. "You're all a bunch of hypocrites."

"If you're so willing to kill her, why didn't you do it that time you were over for dinner?" She had brought him into her house. She hadn't known, hadn't even suspected. She had insisted that he wasn't dangerous.

Her mom had been right to be suspicious.

Jake kept his back to her as he answered. "I should have. I meant to. But when I got there, I... couldn't. I chickened out, and I lost my chance." His voice hardened; his muscles clenched. "I won't make that mistake again."

"You don't have to do this." The words were useless. How could she convince Jake that he shouldn't kill her mom when she wasn't even sure she believed it herself?

"Listen to Sarra," his dad urged. "Forget about this."

"Shut up!" Jake yelled. "I have to do this. I'm doing this for you!"

His dad cowered against the wall.

Jake turned back around to face Becca. "Are you going to help me?"

She saw her answer reflected in his eyes before she knew what she was going to say.

"No," she told him. "I'm not."

"Then I'll have to do it on my own." He squared his shoulders. "You were right—we don't have much time left if we stay here. They'll find us soon. But that just means I need to get this done as soon as possible."

Becca tried to speak. But she still didn't know what she wanted to say.

Jake looked at her like he didn't know her. "It's time for you to leave."

She had to stay. She had to convince him not to kill her mom... or help him do what had to be done. She didn't know. All she knew was that she had to stay.

But like a coward, she left.

* * *

Becca sat scrunched against the head of her bed, knees pulled to her chest. Her pillow dangled precariously off the edge, where it had landed when she had shoved it aside. She wrapped her blankets around herself like a cocoon. It didn't help block out the cold. The cold came from inside her; no amount of blankets would help.

Her eyes ached from crying. Her head ached from thinking.

She still didn't have an answer.

She threw the blankets off and left the room, not caring how much noise she made this time. When she reached her mom's door, she hesitated, but only for a second. She pushed the door open and walked in.

The room felt so still that Becca started tiptoeing without realizing it. Was her mom at work already? It had to be almost morning by now. But the bed looked too lumpy to be empty. Becca squinted. No, her mom was still here—lying in bed, curled on her side, the worry lines erased from her face in sleep. As Becca got closer, she stirred. Becca took another step forward. Her mom's eyes snapped open like Becca had tripped some invisible alarm.

Her mom's worry lines etched themselves back into place. With a groan, she pulled herself upright. "What's wrong?"

Becca shouldn't have come in here looking for comfort like a five-year-old after a bad dream. Any comfort her mom could offer would be tainted by what Becca knew about her.

You know what she is.

Becca searched for some excuse she could give for coming in here in the middle of the night, some way to reassure her mom that nothing was actually wrong.

She opened her mouth—and started sobbing.

She couldn't stop the flow. Her legs buckled under her. She collapsed to the floor as her tears fell faster and faster.

Her mom eased herself to the floor beside her. She didn't say anything. She just wrapped Becca in her arms, the way she had held her when she really had been a five-year-old with a bad dream, the way Jake had comforted her at the playhouse earlier. Becca knew she should pull away, get away from the blood on her mom's hands. Instead she sank into the comfort her mom offered.

She felt a little warmer.

"I don't know what to do," she whispered. She hadn't

meant to say it aloud.

"I know," said her mom, just as quietly. "I know how hard it is." She tightened her arms around Becca. "But no matter what Heather and Jake and anyone else have told you, you still know what's right."

"How am I supposed to know?"

"Knowing isn't the hard part." Her mom stroked her hair, like she always used to when Becca was in bed with a fever. She hadn't done that in years. "I know you, Becca. You're smart enough to see through the lies they've been telling you. The hard part comes when you don't want to do the thing you know is necessary."

Turn Jake in so Internal could kill him. Do nothing, and let her mom die.

Whose life was she supposed to trade away?

Her mom spoke softly. "Is there something you want to tell me?"

She had to make the choice that would let her live with herself later. But what if she couldn't live with either choice?

You know what she is. Jake's voice echoed in her mind. Fast behind it came the memory of what her mom had said. *Every day when I look at the dissidents in those cells, I have to remind myself all over again what they are, so that I can do what needs to be done.*

The two blended together until Becca couldn't tell who was saying what.

Until all she could hear was a third voice. Her own.

She didn't want to leave her mom's comfort behind and step back into the cold. But she forced herself to pull away, to push herself up on her shaky legs until she was standing upright again. "I think I need to be alone for a while."

Her mom watched her as she walked to the door.

"Whenever you're ready, I'll be here."

Without her mom's arms around her, the cold enveloped her again. But this time it didn't sink as deeply into her bones.

She knew what she had to do.

chapter twenty

Becca sat beside her bedroom door, her back against the wall, listening. The only sounds she heard were the ever-present electric hum and the faint thumps of her mom getting ready for work. She had been sitting here since she had left her mom's bedroom. She couldn't wait in the living room. If she did, her mom would wonder why she was up so early.

Maybe it wasn't going to happen. Maybe she had put herself through all this for nothing.

She closed her burning eyes. She would just let herself rest for a minute. Just for a minute...

She didn't realize she had fallen asleep until the doorbell woke her.

Her eyes sprang open.

If everything was going the way she had planned, she had

nothing to worry about. But if something had gone wrong...

And it would be so easy for something to go wrong.

She raced out of the room and toward the door—just in time to see her mom reach for the knob.

She couldn't get there in time, couldn't stop her mom from opening the door.

Couldn't stop Jake from walking inside.

He was here.

The smile he had used to lure her in was long gone. His mouth was a straight line, his eyes two stones. She didn't want to look down, but her gaze traveled to his hands, to the gun he clutched like he was afraid it would betray him.

Her mom drew in her breath. She stood like a statue as Jake swung the door shut behind him. "Becca," she said without taking her eyes off Jake, "get out of here."

Becca stepped forward. "You don't have to do this. You can still leave."

"You know why I have to do this." Jake turned to Becca's mom and took a deliberate step toward her. "You know too, don't you? You recognized me when I came over for dinner that night."

"I'm sorry for what happened to you." How could her mom sound so calm? "But if you do this, you'll give up any chance of getting out alive."

"My life doesn't matter anymore. Protecting my dad is all that matters." Slowly, Jake raised the gun. He kept walking, driving Becca's mom back and back until she hit the wall beside the couch. He pressed the barrel of the gun to her forehead. "And he won't be safe as long as you're alive."

No. No. It wasn't supposed to happen this way.

Becca moved forward, toward Jake; she didn't know what

she could do, but she had to do something. Jake held up a hand to stop her. "You stay where you are."

"This won't help protect your father." Becca's mom sounded like they were chatting at the kitchen table or something. Like she didn't have a gun to her head. "If you kill me, Internal will assume he was involved. They'll arrest you both."

Becca crept closer. One tiny step after the other. Jake didn't look at her; his eyes were fixed on her mom.

"You'll kill us anyway. Just like you killed Mom and Sarra." He dug the barrel of the gun deeper into her skin. "I won't let you hurt anyone again."

Becca inched forward. She and Jake were almost close enough to touch.

Jake's hand shook. "You won't hurt anyone again," he repeated.

Her mom's breaths were slow and even. "You don't want to do this." If it had been anyone but her mom, Becca wouldn't have been able to read her well enough to hear the quiver of fear that broke through the mask of calm.

"I have to." Jake drew a shuddering breath. "I have to do this. I have to do this." He repeated it to himself like a mantra.

Another step forward. Close enough to kiss.

Jake still didn't see her.

She jerked her arm out, quick as a striking snake, and wrenched the gun from his hand.

It took her a second to understand that it had worked, that she was holding the gun, that her mom was still breathing.

The gun felt cold and foreign in her hands. She wanted to drop it to the floor. She forced herself not to let go.

Her mom lunged for Jake. Jake shoved her away before she

could touch him. Her head hit the wall with a sickening crack, and she crumpled to the floor.

Had he killed her? No. No, he couldn't have killed her so easily.

Jake's hand was still shaking as he held it out to her. "Give me the gun, Becca. Let me finish this."

"I'm not going to let you kill her." She was surprised by how steady her voice sounded.

There. Her mom's chest moved as she took a breath. The movement was slight, but enough for Becca to see. She was alive.

In that moment of distraction, Jake twisted the gun out of her hands. Before she could even think about trying to stop him, it was gone.

He leveled the gun at her mom.

"I have to do this," he whispered.

There was only one thing Becca could do. Only one choice she could make.

She took a step forward, placing herself between Jake and her mother. She turned to face him.

She tried to ignore the gun pointed straight at her. Tried to ignore the pounding in her chest.

"I won't let you kill her," she repeated.

Jake's hand wavered, but he didn't lower the gun.

She met his eyes. She didn't look away.

She hoped he couldn't hear how fast her heart was beating.

"Leave her. Take your dad and disappear. It's the only way you'll really be able to protect him."

Jake took a shuddering breath. His hand steadied.

The bang made the walls shudder. For one confused second Becca wondered why she hadn't felt the shot. Jake startled;

the gun slipped from his fingers, and Becca realized it hadn't gone off after all. The door had swung open so hard it had slammed into the wall.

They were here. Not too late after all. They were finally here.

Two Enforcers rushed into the room. One tackled Jake to the floor while the other hurried to Becca's mom's side.

They could have been the same Enforcers who had come for Becca a few days ago. Becca couldn't tell. The uniform erased everything else about them.

Becca's mom was sitting upright, one hand holding the back of her head. "I'm all right," she assured the Enforcer who was looking her over for signs of injury. "He didn't have a chance to hurt me. My daughter saved me."

The Enforcer turned to Becca. "You're the one who made the call?" His helmet muffled his words.

She nodded. She didn't trust herself to speak.

He held out his hand for the gun. She gave it to him.

"I hope you understand what you did today," he told her. "Not only have you helped us catch this dissident, you've saved your mother's life."

The other Enforcer hauled Jake to his feet. Jake didn't try to fight. He stared into Becca's eyes, the same searching look he had given her when she had first seen him across the cafeteria. She forced herself not to look away. She had to face what she had done.

If he hadn't come here this morning... if he had just stayed at the playground, or left town... they never would have found him. She hadn't told them where he was hiding.

But she had known he would come.

The Enforcer shoved Jake toward the door. "Move,

dissident."

Jake didn't deserve what they would do to him.

But if she hadn't called Internal, Jake would have killed her mom. Killed her for what she was, just like Becca would have died in 117 for what she was. Would have, if her mom hadn't saved her.

Jake had been right. Becca knew what her mom was.

But she also knew *who* she was.

If Becca could have taken care of this any other way, she would have. But she couldn't stand back and let Jake kill her mom. She had to become somebody she could live with. And she couldn't live with herself if she let people die for *what they were*—dissident, torturer, as though nothing else about them mattered. She couldn't live with herself if she became her mother.

Becca wanted to tell Jake all of this. She wanted to beg him to forgive her, or at least to understand.

But she couldn't say anything without revealing herself as a dissident.

Jake kept his eyes locked on hers as the Enforcers led him out of the apartment, until the doors closed behind them and he was gone.

chapter twenty-one

It hadn't been easy for Becca to get her mom to let her leave the apartment. Now, as she stood with one hand on the rusted slide, she wished her mom hadn't given in.

She took a slow breath. Then another.

She was stalling.

She forced her legs to move. They carried her mechanically through the weeds and into the playhouse.

Jake's dad still hadn't moved. But as Becca walked in, all his muscles tightened; he squeezed himself further into the corner, eyes frantic.

Becca remembered the bruises on Jake's neck that night. What if Jake's dad thought she was from Internal? All her instincts told her to run, but she stayed where she was. "It's okay. I'm here to help you." She kept her voice as soft as possible.

He relaxed a little, but he still had that trapped look in his eyes. "You. It's you." She couldn't tell whether his tone was relief or fear.

She had no way of knowing who he was seeing when he looked at her. But it didn't matter. "It's me." She sank down to the floor, slowly, carefully, until she was sitting next to him.

The smell of this place made her forget, for a second, that any time had passed since her fight with Jake last night. She could almost see him standing in front of her, arguing with her about why her mom needed to die. A tear escaped her eye, burning the raw skin underneath; she wiped it away. More tears threatened behind her eyes. She hadn't thought she had any left in her.

"Do you know where Jake is?" he asked, like his life depended on the answer.

Becca's breath caught. It took her a moment to respond. "You don't need to worry about him right now. There's just one thing you have to do. But it's really important that you do this, okay?"

Some of the fear faded from his eyes. He edged a little closer. "What is it?"

She reached her hand into her pocket, keeping her movements slow, aware of how closely he was watching her and the way he tensed every time she moved a little too fast. She pulled out the strip of paper Jake had given her. It was soft from handling and creased in dozens of places, but the numbers were still legible.

"You need to get to a phone," she told him. "And you need to call this number. It'll put you in touch with the people Sarra was working with. Tell them who you are, and where you are."

So many risks. If he ventured away from the playground, would Internal catch him before he had a chance to find a phone? Would Surveillance overhear the call, and send Enforcement not only for him but for whoever was on the other end of the line? Would the person who answered be willing to help him? But this was all she had to offer. The alternative was leaving him here, stranded, and that wasn't an option. Especially not after what she had done to Jake.

He took the paper and smoothed it between his fingers. "Will they help me find Jake?"

"Don't worry about him," Becca repeated. "Just call that number. As soon as possible. If you don't, Internal will find you."

He shuddered at the mention of Internal.

"Will you do it?" asked Becca.

He nodded. "I'll do it."

She hoped he would make it. She wished she could do more for him. But she had nothing else to give him. She hadn't even been able to bring more food, not with her mom watching her so closely.

She had to get out of here before he asked her about Jake again. "I have to go." But she stayed where she was. There had to be something else she could do for him.

But there wasn't.

"Good luck," she said. She got up and walked to the doorway.

Before she could leave, he spoke again. "Becca."

She stopped.

He knew who she was.

"He's gone, isn't he?" Jake's dad asked quietly.

Becca stood in the doorway, unable to bring herself to answer his question but unable to walk away.

"Yes," she finally answered. "He's gone." Better for him to know the truth than for him to be waiting forever for Jake to come back.

"He wouldn't have given up. He would have killed her no matter what." Now he was the one holding back tears. "I understand. You had to do it. You had to keep your family safe."

"I'm sorry," she whispered.

Her vision blurred as she left the playground for the last time.

* * *

Becca's mom didn't move when Becca walked in. She stayed on the couch, staring out the window—or maybe staring at nothing at all. For a second, she reminded Becca of Jake's dad.

"I'm back," said Becca.

"Good." In that one word, her mom's voice betrayed her exhaustion. Not the simple fatigue Becca saw in her when she came home after working for sixteen hours straight. This was something deeper.

Becca hung back. She eyed the space beside her mom, and then the path that led to her bedroom. She didn't want to do this. It wasn't going to work; how could it possibly work?

But she was going to have to do it sooner or later. No matter how much time her mom spent away from home, Becca couldn't avoid her forever. If this wasn't going to work, better to find out right away.

Her feet dragged as she made her way to the couch.

She sat down next to her mom. "You said you were ready whenever I wanted to tell you what's going on." She didn't have to fake the quiver in her voice. "I'm ready now."

Her mom reached out and took her hand. "I'm listening." Her mom's hand felt like ice against hers.

Becca took a moment to collect her thoughts, to make sure she knew what she wanted to say. "I didn't know Jake was a dissident at first. But he started saying things. Things about the government, and about Internal. I knew I should report him, but I started to believe the things he was saying."

Jake at the playground, screaming about what her mom had done. The night she had found out for sure that he was a dissident. She stopped for a moment as the memory lanced through her.

"When he disappeared, I figured Internal had taken him," she continued, eyes stinging. "Until... well, you know what happened after that." When had it gotten so hard to breathe? "He found me last night. He told me he was going to kill you for what you had done to his family. He... he wanted me to help him."

Where was he now? Staring down at the bloodstain on the floor in the same cell where she had stayed, or in another identical room deep within the underground maze? Was he being interrogated right now? Was he already dead, or would she see him on TV in a couple of weeks, hear his broken voice as he recounted his crimes?

"It's all right." Her mom squeezed her hand. "It's over now."

"When he asked me to help him kill you, it made me see what was going on. What he really was, and what he had been doing to me. I told him I would think about it, and... I called Internal." Even now, she wasn't sure she had done the right thing. But she'd had to do it. In her head, she heard Jake's mantra. *I have to do this.*

"Why didn't you come to me?" Becca couldn't tell what her mom was thinking. "If I had known he was coming, we could have been prepared."

"I didn't want to admit what I had gotten involved in. I figured I'd call Internal, and they'd arrest him, and you'd never have to know." Not true. The Enforcers would have come to the apartment no matter what, since she'd told them she didn't know where Jake was hiding. Even if Jake had decided not to come, her mom would still have found out. But this way she had kept control of the situation for a little longer. She had been able to give Jake more of a chance.

"I didn't think they would take so long," she said. "Maybe they didn't know whether to believe me, because of what happened the other day."

"That sounds about right." Now her mom sounded angry—but not at Becca. Her voice held an ominous bite. "I'll have a talk with whoever was responsible for that decision."

"I didn't mean for any of this to happen. But I get it now. I understand what you were trying to tell me. I'm sorry it took something like this to make me see it. But sometimes your life has to fall apart before you can really see what's important." Becca held her breath, waiting for the inevitable. Waiting for her mom to tell her she didn't believe a word of it.

Her mom dropped her hand and reached her arms out toward her. Becca flinched away. Ignoring her reaction, her mom pulled her into a hug. "It doesn't matter," she murmured against Becca's hair. "You remembered what's right. That's the important thing."

Her mom believed her.

Her mom couldn't see through her lies anymore.

Becca should have been happy. Instead, something deep inside her ached as the last of her old connection with her mom tore away.

Her mom pulled back. "While you were gone, I did some thinking."

"About what?" Becca asked, when her mom didn't keep going.

"About you. About what would be best for you." A long breath. "It may be a good idea for you to go live with your father."

At first Becca thought she must have misheard. But the pain in her mom's eyes told her she hadn't.

"If not for me, Jake wouldn't have used you the way he did," said her mom. "You wouldn't have come so close to becoming a dissident. And I can't stop thinking about what happened this morning—and what could have happened. What if he had shot you first, to take away my family like I took away his? What if the next one gets that idea in his head, and Enforcement doesn't show up in time?"

She could leave here. Leave it all behind—Processing 117, her mom, Heather, the rumors at school, the memory of Jake. All of it. She could push away her dissident thoughts the way her dad had pushed away his, until she started to believe her own lies. Once, she had hated the thought of embracing denial the way he had. Things were different now. She was different now.

"This is your decision," said her mom. "I won't force you to go. But at least think about it. Don't worry about what I want; all I want is what's best for you."

Becca could already taste it. A life away from her mom's

contradictions, away from the shadow of 117.

It tasted like freedom.

She didn't know what to say. "I'll need some time to think."

Her mom nodded. "Of course."

It wouldn't really be freedom. Only denial. Internal would still be there, doing what they always did. Executions would still air on TV. Every so often, someone from school would disappear.

But she wouldn't have to think about it.

It wouldn't be freedom... but wouldn't it be almost as good?

* * *

Becca glanced over her shoulder at the car as her finger hovered over Heather's doorbell. She could still just leave. Go back to the apartment. Help her mom make dinner. Heather probably didn't want to talk to her anyway.

She rang the doorbell.

She didn't even have time to hope nobody would be home before the door opened. Heather's eyes widened before she smoothed her face into a neutral expression. "Becca."

"Can I come in?" Becca asked, feeling absurdly shy in front of the person who had been her closest friend for almost as long as she could remember. "I want to talk to you."

Heather studied her warily.

"I'm not going to hurt you." When had Heather started being afraid of her? "I just want to talk. Really."

Another second of hesitation. "Okay." She held the door open for Becca.

Becca followed Heather up the narrow staircase and into her bedroom. The boxes were gone, all except for one, which Heather had turned on its side to stack her clothes in. The room didn't look like it belonged to the Heather she knew—her textbooks were piled by her bed instead of strewn across the floor, the walls were bare except for a single Internal poster hanging above her bed where a giant collage of her friends had hung in her old room, and there wasn't a dirty sock in sight. But it didn't look temporary anymore either.

In her old room, Heather would have flopped down on the rumpled bed and asked Becca what was wrong. Now the bed was neatly made, and Heather stood stiffly in the center of the room.

Becca couldn't figure out what to do with her arms. She crossed them, clasped her hands in front of her, let them fall to her sides like dead fish. "I just wanted to say that I understand."

Heather frowned. "Understand what?"

Becca stuck her hands in her pockets. That didn't feel right either. "I understand why you reported me. And I can't hate you for it, not after..." *Not after Jake.* "Not now that I've thought about it some more. I would have been scared too." She had traded Jake's life for a torturer's. Could she condemn Heather for, in a panic, trading Becca's life for her own? "So... it's okay. What you did."

"Oh. Thanks." Heather stretched her lips into a smile.

They stood there for a moment, looking at each other. Becca pulled her hands back out of her pockets.

"Was that everything?" asked Heather.

"I guess. Yeah."

Another few seconds of silence.

"I should probably get home," said Becca. "Mom's waiting for me. She came home early, and I promised we'd have dinner together."

She waited for a response. When Heather didn't say anything, she turned around and walked to the door.

"Wait," Heather said as Becca stepped out into the hallway.

Becca stopped.

"I really am sorry. For turning you in like that. You could have died in there." Heather drew in a breath. "I know it's not okay. But thank you for being willing to forgive me anyway."

Becca turned back around. "I really do understand."

"It's not going to happen again." Heather took a step closer. "I know you, Becca. I've known you for a long time. I can see how you've changed. What happened to my parents changed us both. It made me understand what was important in life... but it turned you into a dissident."

Becca's vision darkened. Everything faded out except Heather. Her heart pounded. She had heard the word in school all day, but this was different. Heather had spent so long refusing to accept how Becca had changed. She wouldn't say it now unless she meant it.

"I'm not a dissident."

"Don't lie to me. I know you too well for that." Heather reached for her pin, then stopped. "I know I should turn you in before it's too late. But I can't. After I told them about you, I didn't sleep until I saw you in school that day. I couldn't think about anything but what they must have been doing to you. I can't do that again."

"I'm not—" Becca started again.

Heather held up a hand. "I told you—don't lie to me."

Heather knew. Becca had convinced her mom, but

somehow, Heather knew.

"I meant what I said," Heather told her. "I won't turn you in."

"Thank you." What else could she say? No matter how many times she said she wasn't a dissident, Heather wouldn't believe her.

The silence stretched longer and longer.

"I guess that's it," said Heather.

"I guess so." Becca wished she had something else to say. Some way to revive their friendship. But they had both changed too much. There was nothing there anymore, no friendship to go back to.

"I'll miss you." Heather's smile earlier had been forced, but her look of regret was real.

"I'll miss you too," said Becca as she left the room. She didn't have to say that the old Heather was the one she would miss. She was sure Heather understood.

chapter twenty-two

Becca speared a piece of chicken with her fork and transferred it to her plate. She breathed in and smiled. "This smells great."

"I hope it tastes as good as it smells," said her mom from across the table. "I'm still not sure about this recipe."

Becca spooned rice onto her plate from the serving bowl. She nudged the edge of the bowl by accident, and it shifted slightly, almost knocking her plate to the floor. She stabilized it just in time. "You don't have to try so hard, you know."

Her mom studied her chicken. "What do you mean?"

"You know what I mean. The special dinners, the movie nights, all the calls from work you've been ignoring..." Becca didn't know whether her mom was doing it to convince her not to go live with her dad, or because she was worried that Becca would turn into a dissident again the second she let her out of her sight. Either way, the end result was the same—Becca and her mom hadn't spent this much time together since Becca was in elementary school.

Her mom still hadn't seen through her lies. Maybe she and her mom really were that distant from each other now… or maybe her mom was just desperate to see what she wanted to see.

Just like Becca had kept herself from seeing the truth about her mom for so long.

Her mom changed the subject. "How did school go today?"

"The same as ever." Becca shrugged. "Maybe a little better. I got through the entire morning death-threat-free, and some freshman I don't even know came up to me in the hall and told me that no matter what anyone else thought, he knew I was a loyal citizen." She pushed her food around on her plate. "Of course, then he asked if I thought you could get him a job in Processing after he graduates."

Over the past six weeks—ever since Jake's arrest, ever since her mom had started spending every spare minute with her—they'd been talking again. Not like they used to; it would never be like it used to be. But Becca could tell her mom things again. She could look at her and almost see the person she used to know.

She hadn't forgotten what her mom was. She didn't try to push it out of her mind anymore; that didn't work. She saw it, and she hated it… but she saw her mom, too.

There were only two things her mom never brought up: Becca's time as a dissident, and the choice Becca still had to make.

"You know I feel about Heather," said her mom, "but—as much as it pains me to say it—you may want to consider following in her footsteps. You said things got a lot easier for her after she joined the Monitors." She began cutting her chicken into neat squares. "Besides, it would be a good step for you if you change your mind about getting a job with Internal after you graduate. I know how you feel about that idea now, but…"

"But things change," Becca finished. "I know. I've been thinking about it."

"About the Monitors, or Internal?"

"Both, I guess. I don't know." Becca took her first bite of chicken. "Hey, this is really good."

Her mom followed her lead. "You're right—this did come out well. Much better than I expected."

Enough dancing around what she needed to say. Enough telling herself she had to think about it some more. She was as sure as she was going to get.

She set her fork down. "So… I made a decision."

She saw the instant her mom realized what this had to be about, saw her face freeze into a mask of resigned acceptance as she prepared for the worst.

It wasn't too late. She could still change her mind.

She spoke before she could give in to her doubts. "I'm not leaving."

Surprise replaced resignation, followed by joy—but only for a second. "Are you sure about this?"

She still had a chance. She could leave all this behind and never look back.

"I'm sure. Living with Dad might be easier—but this is my home. I belong here with you."

Her mom smiled. "If you're sure you've thought it through, then of course I want you to stay." Her smile grew broader, crinkling the skin around her eyes. "I would have missed you."

Mentally, Becca shook away the last of her regrets. This was the right decision. *No matter how hard it gets.*

Her mom raised her fork to her lips—and let it hover there as her phone buzzed.

"You can answer it, you know," said Becca.

Her mom hesitated. "Are you sure?"

Becca nodded. "I told you, you don't have to try so hard."

Her mom put her fork down and answered the phone. "Raleigh Dalcourt." She got up from the table and left the kitchen, murmuring in a low voice.

After a moment, her mom returned. "A new batch of dissidents just came in, and they may have connections inside Internal. The directors want them dealt with as soon as possible." She paused, looking apologetic.

"It's okay," said Becca. "Go."

"I don't know when I'll be back. Probably not until tomorrow."

"I told you, it's okay. Really." Becca smiled. The smile almost felt real. "Go on. They need you."

Becca finished her chicken as her mom gathered her things and prepared to leave. Now that she had made her decision final, she could do what she had been thinking about doing for the past six weeks. With her mom gone, she would have no reason to put it off. No excuses for putting it off.

Her stomach tightened as her mom closed the door behind her.

After she had scraped the last bit of sauce off her plate, she wrapped her mom's almost-full plate of food in plastic wrap and stuck it in the fridge, then put the rest of the leftovers away. She washed the dishes by hand, scrubbing each plate and bowl and piece of silverware until they gleamed. When she was done, she squinted at each clean dish, searching for specks she might have missed.

Stalling.

The dishes were cleaner than they had been when they were new. Becca looked around the kitchen for something else she could wash. She couldn't find anything.

She left the kitchen and walked to her bedroom as slowly as she could without moving backward. Even though she was alone, she closed the door behind her. She sat down at her desk and told herself to quit stalling. It was time. It was past time.

She opened the bottom drawer and flipped through the papers there until she found it. The note she and Heather had found three months ago.

Only three months? It felt like a million years.

Heather's dad's barely-legible handwriting filled most of the page. At the bottom, in Becca's much-neater writing, was a phone number. The number Jake had given her.

She almost shoved the paper back into the drawer. Instead, she spread it out on the desk in front of her.

She had to do this.

In all other ways, she refused to take her mom as an example... but on one thing, they could agree. *I will not be someone who abandons my principles as soon as they become inconvenient. I will not be someone who says that certain things have to be done... as long as somebody else does them.*

She had to do this. No matter how afraid she was.

No matter how hard it gets.

She picked up the phone and dialed.

about the author

Zoe Cannon writes about the things that fascinate her: outsiders, societies no sane person would want to live in, questions with no easy answers, and the inner workings of the mind. If she couldn't be a writer, she would probably be a psychologist, a penniless philosopher, or a hermit in a cave somewhere. While she'll read anything that isn't nailed down, she considers herself a YA reader and writer at heart. She lives in New Hampshire with her husband and a giant teddy bear of a dog, and spends entirely too much time on the internet.

For more information about Zoe Cannon's books and to sign up for updates on new releases, visit http://www.zoecannon.com

You can also find Zoe on Facebook: http://www.facebook.com/ZoeCannonAuthor

On Twitter: http://www.twitter.com/cannonzoe

On Goodreads: http://www.goodreads.com/zoecannon

Or email her directly at zoe@zoecannon.com.

acknowledgements

Thank you to my amazing husband, for giving me the opportunity to live the life I've always wanted, understanding me better than I had thought possible, and offering more unconditional support than I could ever hope to repay;

to my parents, for being nothing but supportive toward my writing endeavors (the more I hear other people's horror stories, the more I realize how lucky I am), and for not being offended at my writing a book called *The Torturer's Daughter*;

to Holly Lisle, for her brilliant How to Revise Your Novel course, which turned this from a bunch of characters and a premise into an actual novel;

to my writing group, for their insightful comments, semicolon-counting, and patience at waiting a year and a half to find out what happened next;

to all the friends I made playing Rift (and especially my favorite fashion-conscious necromancer), for keeping me sane during the Writer's Block From Hell;

to the pioneers of indie publishing for opening up a new way for writers to get their books out into the world, and all the other YA dystopian authors out there for creating a market for my unmarketable stories;

and to Akasha, my monstrous cuddlefiend of a dog, for always being up for a snuggle break and only grumbling a little when I spent too much time on writing and not enough time on belly rubs.

20747113R00157